THREE ANGRY WOMEN AND A BABY

A Heart Warming Feel-Good Romantic Comedy

KERRIE NOOR

CONTENTS

PROLOGUE

Beatrice looked at her phone, then nudged George. "All systems go," she said.

George flicked on the light. "What?"

"It's happening."

"What's happening?"

"The baby," said Beatrice.

"Now—in the middle of the night?" said George.

"Yes. That's when babies come, in the middle of the night."

George pulled a face. "But we don't have to get up, do we? I mean, what are you going to *do?*"

"Be there," said Beatrice.

"Where, Glasgow?"

"She's having a home birth," said Beatrice.

"No one has a home birth in Ardrishaig, it's the middle of nowhere."

"Well, she might."

"She never talked about it."

"Look, just get me there," said Beatrice.

George looked at Beatrice. *Is she calm-able?*

He took a chance.

"The last thing she needs is you in the way. Steven will call us."

Beatrice grunted and pulled her wheelchair closer to the bed.

"What are you doing now?" snapped George.

"I can't sleep," said Beatrice.

"Here, let me," said George.

"No, it's all right, wouldn't want to disturb your sleep. I can do it."

"I said let me," said George.

Beatrice pulled the chair closer, overbalanced, and fell off the side of the bed onto the floor with one leg inelegantly tangled in the sheets.

She tugged at her leg.

"Told you," said George.

"No you didn't," snapped Beatrice.

Sheryl looked at her baby and didn't feel anything. She knew she was supposed to feel *something*, but she felt nothing.

Steven kissed the top of her head and looked at his wife. "She's beautiful."

Nothing.

He kissed the baby's head and then hers again.

"My beautiful wife."

Nothing.

She wanted to cry. Instead, she sighed. *Maybe I'll feel . . . when I get home.*

Sheryl passed the baby to Steven.

"You think of a name. I need some sleep."

The nurse looked at Steven. Sheryl, clocking the look, let out another sigh and rolled over.

Steven, with his precious bundle in his arms, walked to the window. It was like he was in a film. He was so happy—a beautiful baby girl, just like Sheryl. He stared down at her delicate features: the tiny fingers, the button nose. He slid a finger into her hand and her pink fingers curled around it. She was so small.

He stared into the morning sun, drinking in the fragrance of a newborn. "Our first day together, honey."

He turned to look at his delicious wife, her curved back to him. The nurse threw a *she's tired* look.

"There's plenty of time for names," he whispered to his daughter, "isn't there, sweetie?"

Sheryl snored.

Sheryl spent the next day in bed trying not to think about the package in the cot beside her. When the package cried, the nurse picked it up, and Sheryl feigned sleep.

"She's hungry," said the nurse.

Sheryl wiped her eyes open and looked at the tiny face. *I want to feel something, but I can't.*

A middle-aged woman patted her on the arm. "That's right, make the most of the time in here. You'll need it once you get home."

"Aye, that's right," said a young woman in the next bed, "it'll be weeks before you get a night to yourself."

"Well, I wouldn't say that," said the nurse.

"You feeding the wee one yourself?" said the young mother.

Sheryl nodded.

"Make that months," she said.

Chapter One

SHERYL

A stitch in time saves bugger all.

"I hear you're a belly dancer," said the consultant. "Been doing it long?"

"Ten years," I muttered, closing my legs.

He covered me up with a tap on my knee. "That explains it."

"What?"

"You got hips that expand like a snake's jaw," he said, laughing. "You could swallow a car."

The doctor chuckled as I glared at him with my best *is that supposed to be funny?* look. My fanny had had more viewings than a house auction with instruments that would scare a masochist, and I was supposed to enjoy a stupid joke?

"Car," I said with an angry tug at my sheet. "And what size we talking of—mini, four-wheel-drive, limo?"

The doctor flicked his gloves from his hand and tossed them in the bin. "Sense of humour, very good." He smiled, muttering something about my ability to close like a clam.

I was in the middle of a large birthing room with a door that swung open at a whisper of a wind and a foghorn-voiced doctor shouting out the size of my pelvis at a volume that I was sure even the café across the road could hear.

I glared as the consultant lathered his hands under the tap, pulled a towel from the holder, and, without looking at me, continued on about dilations and the like. The two nurses nodded while the teenage-looking students took notes. They didn't look old enough to watch a porn film, let alone handle a dilator.

According to the nurse, he—the consultant—was eccentric, and I was to take any so-called joke with a pinch of "whatever." It was one of the first things she said when I arrived, along with "get undressed," "put this on," and "we need a specimen."

"A while yet," he muttered to the older nurse.

I watched him leave, his white coat flowing like he was a caped crusader, his porn virgins following.

"Snake jaw," I said. "What sort of friggin' bedside manner is that?"

"He's Polish," said the older nurse, like somehow that explained something.

"Polish?" I muttered. "What's that got to do with parking cars?"

"He always talks about cars," muttered the younger nurse.

The older nurse smoothed down my sheet. "But he is the best. Honestly, if I were having a baby, he's the man I'd want." She looked at the younger nurse. "His episiotomies are talked about for months."

"Seamless," said the younger nurse.

I gulped. "Cuts . . . down there?"

"But don't panic." The older nurse patted my arm. "He hardly does them."

"He's more a caesarean guy, very safe," said the younger nurse.

I looked at Steven, who had just entered. "Caesarean?" I yelped. "But I did yoga and breathing."

"Honey, you have the best, he's very good. Parking cars is just his way of lightening the mood."

"Parking cars?" Steven looked at me, confused.

"Mood lightening?" I turned to Steven. "Apparently, talking about my bits like I'm a garage will have me laughing through my labour."

"It's to take your mind off things," said Steven with an *is she okay?* look at the nurse.

"Take my mind off things? That's like saying hit your head against the wall and you won't feel any pain when they cut your peri-fucking-neum."

"Let's just leave the perineum out of it," muttered Steven.

I let out a manic laugh that even I didn't recognise; my moods were seesawing all over the place.

"My mother's been going on about my perineum for months, ever since I told her I was pregnant," I joked.

Steven rolled his eyes. "She mentioned it a few times."

"'Olive oil and rubbing,' she says, 'will keep you like a virgin.'"

Steven threw a look at the older nurse. "She never said that, your mum doesn't believe in virgins."

"Steven hasn't fried anything for weeks." I laughed again and then burst into tears. "My mother's put him off olive oil for life."

Steven looked from one nurse to another, mumbling something about medication.

"Medication? That's your answer to everything," I snapped.

"Well . . . it might help, the breathing certainly isn't."

"Well, you're not trying to push out a tow truck though a pinhole, are you?" I snapped.

"Perhaps it's time for some more medication," muttered the older nurse.

Hours ago, excited, happy, and enthusiastic for a deliciously simple natural birth, I had been whipped into a labour room and given a gown the size of a napkin which hardly covered my breast.

"Is this for nose blowing?" I laughed.

The nurse, a young woman who was bustling in the corner with instruments, laughed out loud. "No dignity in this place," she said.

"It's like a doll's dress," I said, causing more giggles, until the older nurse entered.

"Having babies is no laughing matter," she said to me, "it's serious."

She eyed me, perched on a bedpan like a buoy in the water. "You done anything in that pan yet?"

I mentioned something about waiting for everyone to leave, sending a series of tuts from the older nurse.

Apparently, I had the consultant of all consultants and should be poised for inspection like a cow waiting for an insemination.

"You're lucky he's on tonight," she added before leaving.

The door swung open. I stared into the corridor, grateful it was empty. Perched on a bedpan is not something you want anyone to see.

When I discovered I was pregnant, I was so excited, so happy. Steven had bought a pregnancy test, and as we looked at the blue marker, he cried. We had wanted a baby for so long.

I prepared myself for my birth with yoga moves, belly dancing, and birth classes, rubbing oil on bits and pieces while visualising me glowing with a baby in my arms, Steven beside me, and whale music in the background.

Nothing is funny when you are having a baby. No one tells you how scared you become, how despite the whole world and its dog in the room with you, you are on your own. And no matter how many hold your hand, rub your back, and tell you "you're doing great," you are scared, petrified, that along with the baby, all your innards are going to burst out onto the table, the floor, and even the walls, and you'll never be able to shit on your own again.

When my daughter arrived, Steven punched the air like a football player, kissed me a thousand times, and then punched the air again.

I felt nothing but a huge desire to sleep and was just in the process of doing so when I felt a burning poker sear into the flesh somewhere down below.

I jolted.

My legs were spread out like a dissected frog, the consultant was playing cross-stitch with my bits below, while my daughter was being attended to under a chorus of "she's lovely," "she's beautiful," and "so like her dad."

"Keep still," snapped a male voice.

I did my best, gritting my teeth with each tug as Steven told the world and my mother that our baby girl was apparently the image of him.

"Yes, all fingers and toes," he laughed. "And Sheryl? Yes, she's fine, waiting for her tea and toast."

When it was over, I, sipping the best tea I had ever tasted in my life, cracked a joke about tapestry and how my husband would appreciate the artistic display next time he was "down there."

The consultant flicked off his gloves and moved to the sink. I was just about to sink my teeth into my toast when he, without looking up, said, "Don't I know you?"

I looked at the nurses, then Steven. *Know me?* I mouthed. *The only thing he's seen is my fanny.*

"Don't worry," said the young nurse. "He says that to all the girls."

"He's Polish," added the older nurse.

Chapter Two

STEVEN

Great sex comes when you least expect it.

Turns out the consultant did know me, or rather he recognised me, and I wasn't sure it was a compliment or not. He had remembered me from ten years ago in Glasgow, where my dancing, according to him, had inspired his daughter.

Did I look that bad ten years ago, or did I look that good after having a baby?

The notion had me staring into my tea until the older nurse kindly explained he had recognised me from my notes.

"And here's me thinking I hadn't aged." I laughed out loud and yet again burst into tears.

Ten years ago, I performed in Glasgow and also saw Steven in his boxers for the first time. I ripped them off in a frenzy of lust and wine and he had to eat his fry-up in commando the next morning, which we both found strangely erotic.

In fact, for the next few years, everything was erotic to us, from dipping strips of bread into a boiled egg to polishing a doorknob; one look a mundane task could send us searching for the great underrated "quickie."

That night, in my hotel room, Steven declared that I was his muse, his best friend, and that life without me was not worth living. We had emptied the complimentary drink cabinet at the time, which was enough to make a packet of out-of-date peanuts taste like luxury and removing a coin belt as difficult as untangling a wool ball.

"Never try to strip with a coin belt," I laughed, unhinging it from my bra. "It catches everything."

Steven wrapped it around his boxer shorts and managed a few pelvic thrusts that had me ripping his boxer shorts off and tossing them in the bin. All those hours of waiting and eye contact. He was like a present sitting under a Christmas tree—waiting to be opened.

That night, as the whole world (well, Glasgow) celebrated Nefertiti's dancing, Steven walked me back to our hotel and never left my room.

Nefertiti, my belly dancing teacher, had pulled a group of us together and called us the Sisterhood. Our first performance was in Glasgow. For me, a tubby woman who didn't like being seen in a bathing suit, let alone showing my belly, it was a liberating experience that set my libido soaring. Hips circling can do that to a girl, especially in front of a cheering audience in a costume that would make Miss Piggy shaggable. We had been practicing for months, and on the big day, Steven, who was in charge of driving, had the journey planned, with freshly ground coffee, herby baguettes filled with salad and cheese, and some yoghurt to follow.

"Something light," he said, "before the performance."

How could a woman turn down a homemade herby baguette? Especially when feeling like the Queen of Sheba?

We danced to drums, and I, in the front, was, for one song, the main event. The funny thing was, the only person I saw was Steven.

His warm body took me by surprise. We laughed and talked on a creaky bed that rocked with each movement and a headboard that crashed against the wall louder than any moans. We messed up the bed and caused mass destruction in the bathroom and laughed until we fell asleep.

I forgot about the moaning and the rattling bedhead until the next morning, when Steven, sitting uncomfortably in his jeans dipping bread into his fried egg, was asked by the waitress if he had "slept well?"

The old man at the next table glared over his scrambled egg, then muttered to his wife, "Sleep well? This place is like a knocking shop with friggin' tissue paper for walls."

Within a year, Steven had moved in, helping to set up my "no job too small" DIY business. I was living in a converted garage in my mother's garden. It had been converted on the cheap; I hadn't planned to stay long. Ten years later, staring at the blue strip of the pregnancy test, Steven looked about the tiny sitting-room-come-kitchen-come-pull-out-bed-bedroom and muttered about moving.

Moving from my mother wasn't easy—she liked us there. Her and George had an ongoing on/off sort of relationship.

To be honest, I was surprised there was ever any on; she was unbelievably hard to live with. Mum was uncompromising on all fronts, from breakfast to the remote; everything was a minefield with her.

"Don't burn the toast."

"You call this cooked?"

"Coffee, no sugar, just a hint of milk—no, not heated, *warmed*."

George, a patient man with an excellent sense of humour, had a tendency to leave and not come back for days. He called it "downtime." He had two sets of toothbrushes, a selection of PJs—in fact, two of everything. However, Mum didn't like being alone. She, for all her claims to "love" her independence, liked someone within yelling distance. She hated wheeling herself out of the house unaccompanied. She liked to know, as she put it, that if she overbalanced in her wheelchair, someone was just a shout away.

She had no truck with the so-called care in the community; as she said, "the council is full of tits and arseholes" (she always reverted to body parts when angry) and "I'm not spending an afternoon on the floor waiting for someone to answer my friggin' buzzer."

We looked at the blue line of the pregnancy-testing kit, still trying to take it in.

"Steven," yelled Mum. "Don't forget to take the bin out."

"We really need to move," he said.

Chapter Three

MUM

A hammer is only as good as its holder.

We had tried to move several times over the years, but something always got in the way, mainly Mum. Mum objected to all the houses we saw: she would wheel into our bedsit, spy the latest leaflet, and pooh-pooh it with as many reasons why not as she had stories.

Soon, what would be wrong with the next place became a joke between us . . . until I fell pregnant. Suddenly, there was little to laugh at.

George maintained that Mum meant well. My sister, however, saw it differently.

She laughed her head off. "You'll need to give up the booze," she said, wiping tears from her eyes.

Like I drank every day . . .

Then she stopped mid-chuckle and looked from me to Steven with a *you poor cow* look.

"What about Mum—have you told her?" said Lindsey.

Steven sighed. "I think she suspects."

"What?" I said.

He looked at me. "Every time she's here, you're throwing up."

"Nothing new there," muttered Lindsey.

"I haven't had a hangover in ages," I snapped.

"And," said Steven, "she's obsessed with your perineum."

Lindsey pulled a face. "Typical . . . has she brought you rich tea biscuits yet?"

Steven looked at me with a *has she?* look.

"Well, yes," I muttered.

"Bugger," muttered Lindsey, "it's worse than I thought. She'll want to *help* next."

"You *are* joking," said Steven. "Beatrice helping?"

"You have no idea what is coming," said Lindsey. "The depths of Mother's seduction."

I almost laughed. *Mum, seducing?*

Lindsey threw me a *not kidding* look. "One whiff of baby powder and Mum is unstoppable." She turned to Steven. "She's like a drug addict—she can't get enough of a baby."

"I find that hard to believe," said Steven. "Your mother hates kids. According to her, our moving out of the garage is the event of the century."

Lindsey sniffed. "Mere empty words. Mum's as cryptic as a *Guardian* crossword; she has more double meanings than a Shakespearean play."

"Aren't we being a tad dramatic?" said Steven.

"Dramatic," said Lindsey with a look of impeding plague. "You're like lambs to the slaughter."

Distant memories of when Lindsey was a new mother came flooding back. Within a week of her son being born, Mum had pushed my sister to the brink. Lindsey started phoning me with threats of "wrist-slitting" and "no longer being responsible for her actions."

And Lindsey hated the sight of blood . . .

In the end, my sister survived by moving away and paying a cleaner/babysitter who, to quote both the cleaner and Lindsey, not only knew "all about babies" but gave Mum "a run for her money."

"She'll tempt you, but don't be fooled. And don't let her talk you out of moving." Lindsey grabbed my arm. "Promise me."

I tentatively withdrew my arm. "You make motherhood sound like an execution. Do you have to be so brutal?"

"*Brutal* doesn't even begin to describe motherhood and babies. Tell me you're moving."

"Definitely," muttered Steven.

After Lindsey left, making us promise to "get out while you can," Mum called me over.

I walked in on Mum mid–coffee plunging, humming like a half-cut hairdresser. She gleefully offered cream; I started to feel nervous. She never offered me cream, stating that it was the last thing my hips needed.

I pulled up a seat in the kitchen, catching sight of three books on the table: *Chicken Soup for Grandmothers*, *Natural Childbirth—God's Greatest Gift*, and *There Is More to Babies Than Nappies*.

She offered me one of my favourite chocolate biscuits. "Help yourself," she said with what I presumed was her seductive look. "Keep your strength up."

I eyed her offerings.

She nudged the biscuits towards me.

"So what's your sister saying then?"

I pushed the packet back towards her.

"She had morning sickness too, you know," said Mum.

"Everyone knows about rich tea biscuits," I said.

"Well, you didn't," said Mum.

"Yes I did, I was just being polite," I said.

Mum nudged the biscuit nearer with an *it's chocolate, your favourite* look. "You have no idea of what you are letting yourself into," she said.

"I think I do."

"You can't have enough help when you have a baby, and unlike Lindsey, you can't afford help," said Mum.

A sinking feeling hit me like heartburn . . .

"I've got Steven," I said.

"Pfff, he's just the dad," laughed Mum.

"What do you mean, just the dad? The dad is vital, and he intends on being as vital as they come. Every night he talks to my stomach."

"Stomach? What about the nappies?" she said. "Your father was useless."

"They're disposable now, as easy to slip on as a sock," I said. "And besides, Steven's different."

"Sensitive, you mean."

"*Sensitive* is not a dirty word," I said.

"Aye, but where is sensitivity when you're both needing a break?" said Mum. She pulled out another packet of rich tea biscuits and gave me a *Mum knows best* look.

"I'm not feeling sick at the moment," I muttered.

"Like I said, you can't have enough help," said Mum. "I mean, if it hadn't been for me, where would Lindsey be? She forgets."

"I don't think so," I muttered. "Besides, Steven has arranged for Helen to come and help."

"I'm talking of the wee one." She looked at me. "This Helen may be a dab hand at silicone and tiling, but she'll not be much help with a baby."

Helen, a quiet woman who liked smashing things with a hammer, was Steven's sister. And it was Steven's idea for her to help me install a kitchen—a kitchen which, to quote Beatrice, was "perfectly good as it was."

I filled up my coffee and braced myself for some drama as I told Mum that we were planning on moving and getting something bigger, "at least with more than one room."

She stopped in her tracks. "You in a house?"

"What's so weird about that?" I said.

She looked at me with concern. "Cleaning a house is not for everyone, and moving?" She pulled a face. "Very stressful—are you sure you are up for it with all this morning sickness?"

"We live in a bedsit the size of a tent," I said. "We need more room."

Mum slid a chocolate biscuit between her lips, spotting George as he entered. She nodded. "I understand."

"What?" I choked on my coffee.

"And I can help." She paused, catching a look from George. "With the move, that is."

I looked at her. Did she mean it, or was she joking? I hadn't a clue, and I was so confused I dunked a tea biscuit in my mother's coffee. Her lips tilted into a smile.

Chapter Four

HENRY

It takes two years and a TV remote to know the dark side of a partner.

Helen was a woman people didn't notice much, except for Steven. He cared about his sister.

"All's she needs is liberation from that dick of a husband," he used to say, and when I met her husband, I understood why.

Helen was still married to Henry when I first met her. We were sitting in their lounge room a week after our wedding, holding hands as Henry lit the fire. Henry was fresh from the pub and smelt of whisky, while Helen was in the kitchen doing something, according to Henry, "stupid with lentils."

At the time I didn't take any notice of her or her lentils. I was loved up and just wanted the visit to end. Henry was not an easy man to be around. He filled the room with his presence, demanding attention, and I got enough of that from my Mum.

He, like me, worked with his hands; he was a builder who looked at my DIY business as a wee project, a sideline. The last thing you need when you're starting out, especially when your husband buggers off to help his sister with her lentils.

"Any time you need help with your wee project, just let me know," he said, sucking on a roll-up. "Helen don't mind me helping."

Wee project? I wanted to slap his whiskery chin.

"Built this house, you know, when *she*"—Henry tilted his head to the kitchen—"fell pregnant."

He lit the fire, poured himself a whisky, then, with a sip, stared at the flames.

I lingered over my wine. As Henry talked of how he converted the stone byre, into a home.

I could hear Steven and Helen talking cookery, joking.

He looked at me with an "it's all her fault" nod at the kitchen. "Spent my savings on this place. Not that I had much back then, just starting out like you—then *she* gets pregnant . . ."

Helen's laughter filtered from the kitchen.

"Don't get me wrong, I'd love a tribe of kids, a houseful"—he shrugged—"but she can't even cope with one." He shrugged again. "What can you do?"

I didn't know what to say. I mean, I hardly knew the guy, and there he was spilling his guts like a soap opera.

Henry crunched his roll-up between his fingers, tossed it at the fire, and emptied his glass.

"How's that soup coming along, luv?" he shouted. He smiled at me again like a schoolboy. "Hope you're not hungry. She takes ages."

He filled his glass and sipped it like it was the best whisky ever.

"And it's always tasteless. She means well, but Jesus . . ." He shrugged, this time with an excellent *poor me* look. "What can you do?"

He tapped my hand. "But mind, if you need any help . . . don't worry about Helen."

I looked around at the stone walls, dusty, unfinished, littered with roll-up cigarette stubs like a gigantic ashtray, the second-hand furniture that deserved burning, and a pile of tools neatly stacked in the corner.

It was hardly home, it was more a DIY shed.

Really?

He drained his glass like it was tea going cold, then began to tell me what it was like to have a "village idiot of a wife."

"Hormones," he said, "hers are fucked."

I said nothing.

"And I have to deal with everything—even *the talk*."

"Talk?" I said.

"You know, *the* talk," he said.

I looked at him.

"With the daughter," he said, like that made it clear.

Helen popped her head around the corner with a *what's he saying now?* look. She was like a female Steven: blonde wavy hair and so slight that one sneeze would blow her away. Fragile maybe, but not an idiot; in fact, as I was to discover, she had more layers than a puff pastry.

She smiled a Steven smile at me. "Don't take any notice, he always talks too much after the pub."

Henry threw her a "shut it" look.

"Soup's ready," shouted Steven.

I thought the soup was all right—not as great as Steven's enthusiastic, lip-smacking "terrific," but not as bad as the "dishwater" Henry had made it out to be and certainly better than mine. Henry, however, spent the whole meal pulling *I told you it was shit* faces at me like the others weren't there; then, when finished, he wiped the bowl clean with his bread and, with a smile at Helen, said, "The best soup ever," followed by a wink at me.

"Remember, anytime you need help." He smacked his lips.

"Help?" said Helen.

She looked at me. "Help?"

She turned to him.

He shrugged his shoulders. "You got a roof over your head."

"But what about all the other stuff?" She sighed. "All those promises of sorting things later."

She cleared the plates, headed into the kitchen, and began to crash about.

Steven followed.

"I've got to make money, luv," shouted Henry. "Can't afford to turn down work."

On the way home, I called Henry a prick.

Steven sighed.

"That was the afternoon from hell," I said. "That house is freezing —it's like a shed. Do you know she has no wardrobe? And what's with the stone walls, can't he use an ashtray like everyone else?"

"It's been like that since Helen moved in," said Steven.

"Even the cigarette stubs."

"She hoovers them."

"She should get him to pick 'em up with his tongue."

I pulled into our drive and wrenched the brake on.

"God, I hate him," muttered Steven. "He talks about her like she's a dill, a huge burden that only he could deal with."

I touched Steven's knee. "Promise me you'll never start winking," I said.

He laughed.

In the end, Helen left. She moved into a caravan and even came to one of Nefertiti's belly dancing classes. Some folk were taken aback; they never thought Helen had it in her. Others, like Steven, were relieved.

Henry blamed the menopause and carried on as normal.

"She'll soon come back," Henry told everyone, until she, ignoring all his calls, found a job in a garage and built a porch onto her caravan. Then he began to complain of a broken heart.

"It was the flat tyre that did it," she said. "It changed everything."

We were sitting in the Argyll at the time. I, newly pregnant, was drinking sparkling water, and Mum was on her last mouthful of wine. She stopped. "Flat tyre?"

Helen told us how Henry and she had been heading home after helping Amy, her daughter move to college when her tyre exploded.

"Henry was further on," she said, "his four-wheel drive being way faster than my clapped-out mini. He was in a race to get back for some meeting."

"Meeting on a Saturday?" muttered Mum.

"He went mental," said Helen. "'Of all the places to get a flat, you had to choose here,'" he said. "Like I had exploded the tyre myself. Like I had personally jumped out of the car and blasted it with a couple of hand grenades. He tore into me about how useless I was—'what's the point of having a friggin' jack in your boot if you're not going to use it?'—he shouted . . . until someone stopped to help. Then he was nice . . ."

Mum touched her hand.

". . . friggin' nice."

"Jesus," muttered Mum.

"The funny thing is," said Helen, "he had *told* me not to use it. He said if I ever got a flat to call him, as the friggin' jack was a bastard to use, and unless I knew where to put it I'd fuck the car."

Helen sighed.

"It was a lightbulb moment. If I could learn to change my own tyre, then, well . . . what was the point of Henry?"

Chapter Five

THE HOSPITAL

The mothering instincts are not always immediate.

The day after my daughter was born, I woke to the sound of a clattering trolley, hoovering under the bed, and a crying baby. I eased myself up and stared at the row of babies in the corridor lined up in Perspex bassinets.

"Is that mine crying?" I muttered.

The young mother across from me looked up from her phone. "Nah, the nurse will soon let you know."

I flopped back onto my pillow with a sigh. *God, I ached.* I thought about the toilet and gingerly shifted . . .

I had wanted Steven's baby from the first moment I woke to his sweet face . . . I just assumed that ten years of belly dancing would make the whole thing as easy as slipping off a sock.

Easy—it took *hours*.

My muscles felt like they had been stretched to the limit, and they were throbbing rather than "bouncing back," as Neff claimed.

Ten fucking years of dancing . . .

Nobody told me things could be so painful. My bits hurt like fuck, and the thought of going to the toilet scared the hell out of me.

"I feel like there is a hedgehog between my legs," I said.

The young mother made to laugh, then clutched her stomach in pain. She had yelled so much during her labour her voice was hoarse. In the end, she had had a caesarean.

"I mean, is it all going to drop when I go to the loo?" I said.

A nurse appeared with a cup of pills. She told me not to be so stupid, then handed the young mother her tablets with a "here."

"I can't even cough without my stomach feeling like it's going to rip open," croaked the young mother.

The nurse threw her a look.

"I have a low pain threshold," she said.

"Pfff," said the nurse.

"Seriously, I do. My mother said she couldn't even tap me without me screaming—combing my hair was a nightmare."

"Well, you'll need to get out of bed soon," said the nurse, "before the ward round."

The young mother tossed the tablets down. "Until these babies kick in, I ain't moving."

"Don't let Himself hear you say that. He'll be around here getting you to do sit-ups," said the nurse.

"Himself?" I muttered.

"The consultant."

"That Polish git," muttered the other mother mid drawer rummage. She was tiny, with matchstick legs and whisper-thin arms. She looked like one puff of wind would have her over and another would keep her down.

She looked up, catching a "no" from the nurse.

"Well, thank fuck for that." The tiny one grinned at me. "I mean, what sort of wanker talks about cars when you're having a baby? I could have thumped him . . . in fact, I had to hold the ol' man back . . ."

The nurse interrupted. "It's the head consultant, he has a thing about sit-ups."

"Sit-ups?" said the tiny one. "Jesus, haven't done one in years—how am I to do them with all these stitches?" She looked at me. "Won't they split?"

The nurse muttered something about internal stitching.

"Aye, but they're still stitches, still rip," said the young mother.

"Hardly," muttered the nurse.

The tiny one pulled at her handbag. "You've seen my fags?"

"Take mine," said the younger mother.

The nurse threw a look. "No leaving the room until the ward round has finished."

She made to leave and then stopped.

"And don't let him hear you talk about fags."

"As if," muttered the young mother.

We looked at each other. The two chuckled, followed by an *it hurts* stomach clutching.

"Can't even touch my toes, let alone sit up," muttered the tiny one.

They giggled again, then caught sight of my face. I wanted to cry and was having a hard time hiding it.

"Was it rough?"

"First time?" said the tiny one.

I gulped. "I knew it wouldn't be a breeze, but . . . well, the pain."

"The first is the worst, you get used to it," said the tiny one.

I watched her lift her baby like an expert.

"First? You've had more?" I said.

"Three," said the tiny one.

"Two," said the young mother.

"You don't look old enough to leave school," I muttered.

I began to drift . . . then I heard my name being called with the annoying urgency of my mother.

"Sheryl, you awake?"

Ignoring her, I kept my eyes closed.

"She's knackered," muttered the tiny one.

"Best not to wake her," said the younger mum.

Shake, shake . . .

"Sure you're not awake?" said Mum.

Then she stopped. I heard her move across the room . . .

"Is that yours?" she said.

I opened one eye. My mother was cooing over the tiny mother's baby, and if I had a cup of tea, I would have nearly choked on it.

I eased myself up, as Mum moved on to another baby, tickling her cheek. A habit she had taken to ever since I discovered the blue "yes" line on the pregnancy test.

The nurse appeared with a cup of tablets for me. She helped me sit up as Mum scurried over and looked into the cup.

"Iron? That'll block her up, and that's the last thing she needs."

I closed my eyes. God, I was tired.

My mother didn't budge.

"When's she due for a feed?" she said.

I shrugged.

"Can I feed her?"

I sighed.

"What's her name?"

I told my mother that as Steven was a writer, he could name her; after all, he did it all the time.

"She's not a character in a book," snapped Mum. "I hardly think some American gunslinging outlaw of a name is what we are looking for."

I shrugged again.

"She's your daughter, you should name her."

"Plenty of time," said the tiny mother with a look at me.

"Aye," nodded the young mother.

The nurse wheeled in my daughter, her face scrunched with an *I'm just about to wail* look. Mum's face melted. She slid her finger into my daughter's palm and muttered, "Baby Bea."

Baby Bea blinked at my mum, who, with a girly gasp, scooped her up and began to tell her stories of dragons with an expression that had me annoyed enough to forget my aches.

"We shall fight them on the beaches"—Mum laughed—"in the castles and on the sand."

I pulled a face . . .

"What's up with you?" she said.

"Nothing."

"She's tired," said George, appearing in the doorway.

"Tired? You slept all morning. Come sit up, Baby Bea is gorgeous."

Mum bustled in a way that made me want to slap her.

The tiny mother threw me another comrade look. "It's her first," she shouted, "give her space."

Baby Bea started to cry.

My nipples stung like they had been rubbed with sandpaper.

The nurse looked at the wet marks on my gown, ushered Mum and George out, and pulled the curtain about us. Her face softened as she held the baby close to my chest.

"Mums, huh?" she said.

A tear trickled down my cheek. She pulled a tissue from somewhere and handed it to me.

"If you feed her yourself, no one can interfere."

I muttered an "it hurts."

"You'll soon pick it up," she whispered. "Don't worry."

I slid my daughter onto my breast, braced myself, and cried. All I wanted was for Steven to take me home.

Over the past nine months, my breasts had taken on a life of their own, expanding into sizes I had no idea existed. They swamped me, catching everything I ate like a drip tray. And as for trying to dance with them . . . well, that was something I did in private without a mirror.

My new larger-than-life bras didn't help either. They were more like parachutes than underwear, with straps the width of a table leg ingraining bra strap marks on my shoulders. No lace or frilly bits, just little pockets for my nipples to peek out of for feeding. I felt like a cow.

Of course, in the hospital, trying to contain them was not easy for a novice mum like me. They flopped about like plates of jelly, and when the nurse suggested I may not have enough milk, my mother erupted.

"Enough milk? She's got a dairy in there."

Next thing I knew, I was on a milking machine watching a milky substance fill a clear bottle.

At least it didn't hurt.

The nurse appeared to check things and, with a smile and swoosh of curtains, left.

I stared at the "breast is best" poster—a small-breasted mother looking serenely at her newborn like a Catholic Madonna—and wondered, *If Steven saw me now, would he ever suck on my nipples again?*

Chapter Six

HOMECOMING

Motherhood is as natural as making cheese.

When I arrived home from the hospital, I looked at myself in the mirror and cried. My eyes were puffy, my hair was limp, and my stomach had betrayed me . . .

I still looked pregnant.

For nine months, I had pictured myself sitting by a sunlit window feeding my baby like a serene Madonna, bonding like denture glue.

Nobody told me it would hurt.

That my breasts, with nipples the size of beer mats, would have minds of their own, and that the whole "baby latching onto my nipples" thing would require an entourage of nurses to navigate behind a curtain that flapped open at the mere whiff of a trolley passing.

I just assumed I would know what to do—that the baby would attach as quickly as a bath plug in a plughole. Baby Bea, however, seemed to have the aim of a drunk playing darts for the first time with the wrong set of glasses; getting her to attach was as plausible as my mother balancing on a tightrope.

One crusty old nurse tried to encourage, claiming that breast-feeding was a "piece of piss" and "the best thing since Thatcher's dementia."

"Your womb will squeeze back to the size of a walnut," she said, "while all your bottle-feeding friends will be coughing into their TENA Ladys."

I plonked myself on the couch with exhaustion. TENA Ladys were the last things on my mind; my breast, full of milk, ached. It would soon be feeding time—yet again.

Steven was all gooey with being a father; I wasn't in the door five minutes and he was texting pictures, that is until Baby Bea whimpered a cry, then Steven was fussing like a mother hen.

I felt nothing.

"Do you want me to bring her over?" said Steven.

"Guess so."

Steven watched, fascinated, as Baby Bea and I fumbled to attach. Finally, she closed her eyes and began to suck. I waited . . . once Baby Bea got into the rhythm, the pain subsided.

"It's a miracle," he said.

"You would think," I muttered.

As soon as she was fed, he whisked her off to the library with a "you could do with a rest."

A couple of hours later, he was back loaded with coins. In Scotland, older folk always leave coins with a newborn—bad luck not to.

Steven laughed. "Look," he said, "we've made a fortune. We should have more kids."

When I didn't laugh, he offered to make a coffee.

He didn't even bat an eyelid when I said "decaf" or mutter an "I know" when I said "breastfeeding."

Instead, Steven, with great intensity, frothed some milk, sprinkled chocolate on the froth, and handed me a cappuccino in my favorite cup.

"Biscuit?" he said.

"This is fine," I muttered.

"Cheese and oatcakes?"

"Not just now."

"Not even with tomato?"

"No."

"How about some soup?"

I adjusted Baby Bea to the other breast and shook my head.

He began talking about teaching Baby Bea to ride a bike and use a drill.

I almost smiled. Steven handled a drill like it was alive and about to bite him: switching it on with a jump, like the noise was the last thing you'd expect.

"You can't even use one," shouted Mum, crashing open our door with her wheelchair.

She circled the room.

Steven watched with a disheartened look, muttering something about a house available that would take Mum a morning to drive to, while Mum, not listening to a word, began an incompressible speech about rest, babysitting, and getting back on the horse after a fall.

She looked from Steven to me as if we agreed with her.

I could hardly follow her train of thought.

"Mum, I haven't sipped my coffee yet, and you're talking of horse riding."

"It's a figure of speech," said Mum with a queer look at Steven. "You know what I am on about, don't you? Don't want to let the moss grow and all that."

Steven, with a queer look back, said nothing—his usual response when Mum confused him.

Beatrice wheeled herself to my side and cooed at Baby Bea.

"Any time your mum needs some horse riding"—she winked at Baby Bea—"you and I can play stories."

She looked at me. "I'm here to help."

"Help? You just put her off her feed," said Steven.

"I make coffee, don't I, Sheryl?"

"No," I said.

Steven, without a word, lifted Baby Bea. He had the same expression on his face he used to have years ago when he first started working with Mum, a sort of "marking my territory" expression that, at the time, stopped me in my tracks.

"I am off to the co-op," he said, "in search of the elderly folk and coins."

He jumped into the car with a confidence new to him, while Mum continued on about moss growing and horse riding.

"I take it you're talking about sex," I said, flopping back onto the couch.

Mum never talked of sex without mentioning animals of some sort. When she gave me "the talk," it started with cats and things swinging between their legs—like any teenager would look there.

When I first told Steven about the "sex talk," he laughed his head off. He was as keen on cats as dogs, being that both were in some way reasons for his fear of driving.

Steven used to hate driving; in fact, he would do anything rather than drive. But he was desperate for a baby like me, and as soon as I was throwing up in the bathroom, he was there with a towel and digestive. Then, when the pregnancy test said "yes," he vowed to "take care of the two of us and start driving again."

"I need to get over this whole too-scared-of-the-traffic thing," he said. "I mean, how will we get you to hospital?"

The hospital was only ten minutes away.

He practiced every day, fine-tuning his reverse parking. He manned up to dogs and cats that had terrorized his early driving years, stooping to pat rather than dodge. He even took tips from Mum, which had not only her but just about everyone we knew choking on their coffee.

No one took driving tips from Mum. Most spent their time thinking up excuses for not going in the car with her.

Mum drives like there is a fire and she's the only fireman. She has as much patience and understanding as a toddler.

No one can take a corner like she can; as for swerving, she swears by them, claiming that it keeps everyone on their toes. My mother has written off more cars than McDonald's has hamburgers. She knows all the police by name, and if it wasn't for the fact that she was in a wheelchair and old enough to be their grandmother, I am sure she'd be fined within an inch of her life.

Which is why George now drives, and she sits in the front telling him whichever gear he is in is the wrong one.

George is the sort of driver who eases himself into a car like it's an armchair. He never moans about people forgetting to use their indicator, despite Beatrice attempting a toot with the horn. Instead, he cheerfully waves to everyone, treating long journeys like a safari ride, stopping to take photos of "the wildlife". . . which keeps Mum in total huffing mode, claiming that sheep and the like were "hardly buffalo."

I looked at the empty Baby Bea space. I was a mum with no idea how to do anything and, thanks to my own mum, a good idea what not to do.

I stared out of the window with a flat sense of *Shouldn't I feel something?* as Helen pulled up in our DIY van.

Chapter Seven

HELEN

Jealousy trips you up when you least expect it.

My mother was never one for "mollycoddling," as she put it; she was more a "get on with things" sort of person. A cough got better with fresh air, and there was nothing a bit of starvation wouldn't cure when it came to upset stomachs.

When she first noticed me running to the loo to throw up, she, assuming it was something to do with drink, said little apart from "One too many, Sheryl?"

After a week of this, she changed and began to offer herbals and rich tea biscuits. She brought me packets of both, telling me to "get a few down in the morning, before the sickness kicks in" and began to tell me to "take it easy."

When Helen joined my business, Mum was dubious. I had just found out I was expecting, and she was in panic mode about me scaling ladders while pregnant. The last thing I needed, according to her, was to train someone who was as "wobbly as a plate of jelly."

And Helen could be wobbly. She drove like she didn't deserve a car space, let alone space on the road. Every time a police car siren went by, she panicked thinking it was her; she wore guilt like a cloak.

Mum said it was living with *him* that did it, the "constant criticism made her a nervous wreck. But as we worked together, Mum began to warm to her.

We fixed leaky roofs, dug drainpipes, and installed a new kitchen. Helen was as helpful as Steven's back rubs and as kind as he was, reassuring me that the heartburn would go away and my body would shrink back to its normal size. She rarely got angry, loved helping people, and had all the time in the world for old folk, even when they jumped the queue.

Mum began to wave her up for coffee and entertain her with quirky "Sheryl stories," which, Helen, to give her her due, listened to with a noncommittal face.

By the time I was six months pregnant and "blooming like a beached whale," Mum's conversations revolved around Helen, which Helen seemed oblivious to and I was completely fed up hearing.

As I spent more time getting my breath back, easing myself out of the van, or reminding my foggy brain with lists, Helen slowly took over, finishing things before I even had a chance to start them. I mean, she wasn't a know-it-all like her older sister or bossy like the youngest. Helen was nice, efficient, and quiet, and she always talked to me like we were a couple of blokes; mummy stuff rarely left her lips.

Helen was . . . well . . . annoyingly good. In fact, I couldn't bleeding well fault her.

Soon, the only thing Mum wanted to talk about was Helen, her "bad egg of a husband," and her marvelous ability to fix things without *one* swear word.

In Mum's eyes, any man that drove about in a personalized number plate was the equivalent of a gangster. Henry's four-wheel drive with HEN69 really got up her nose, that and the need for a stepladder to get into it . . .

Even when I tried to change the subject, she still continued on about Helen and her arsehole of an ex.

Once Mum was so intent on finishing her story she followed me to the loo, shouting outside the toilet door how Henry had called Helen a "half-wit" at the butcher's.

"Mum, do we have to talk about him again?" I said, flushing the toilet.

"She's just too easygoing for her own good," said Mum, like she hadn't said that a million times.

I opened the door and practically tripped over Mum.

"Has he seen her on a roof?" said Mum without moving.

I eased myself and my bump past.

"I mean, that woman is like Spiderman."

"I've been on a few roofs too, you know," I said.

Mum, feigning deafness, followed me into the kitchen and flicked on the kettle.

"We don't have time for coffee," I said. The thought of it made me want to balk.

Mum, still feigning deafness, pulled coffee from the cupboard and began to circle the kitchen for milk.

"I don't know why you're getting so het up, he's not your husband," I said.

Mum, now engrossed in mug searching, began to mutter like I wasn't even there.

"Slap a bit of writing on the side of your gangster car and people think you're a big man . . ."

"There's writing on the side of my van," I shouted.

"I know, dear," said Mum still in search of mugs, "but it's hardly an impressive van is it?"

I jumped as Mum wheeled herself inches from my toes, pulling open a cupboard.

"Where's Helen?" she said.

"Emptying the unimpressive van," I snapped.

Mum peered out of the window and watched Helen slide a couple of pipes from the back of the van like she was lifting a crisp packet.

"She's some woman," muttered Mum.

I huffed.

"One of Steven's better ideas," she said.

I looked at Mum. "I lift pipes too, you know."

Mum eyed me. "In that state? I hope not."

"I'm not *sick*," I said.

Mum didn't hear; she was busy waving a "you want a coffee?" wave.

"I told you, Mum, we have no time for coffee." I closed the mugs cupboard. "Pipes don't get laid on their own."

Mum looked at me and, with an annoying ruffle of my hair, let out a loud laugh. "You and your pipes—you can hardly lay one now."

Chapter Eight

THE LIBRARY

Getting the better of a bully is as exhilarating as a tax return.

I never for a moment saw myself with Steven; he was a man who seemed ineffectual. How wrong I was—he was anything but ineffectual. I mean, he not only put up with my mother, he managed her.

Steven ran the library like an expert. He made it the hub of the community, and his quirky Westerns were part of that hub. People loved being served by an author; even Mum sprouted on about his books, not that she had read any. In fact, she banged on about his books almost as much as her retiring and what she would do if she didn't have to "run this place" (meaning the library).

According to her, the only thing that was stopping her leaving was the library's inability to function without her, like she had personally built it, bought the books, and paid the rent.

Steven sussed her out within the first week of stamping books alongside her, but then he is a writer, an expert of human nature. People come to the library just to confide in him. What he doesn't know about humans is not worth knowing; he makes a physiologist look like an agony aunt.

Steven managed Mum like a sheepdog with sheep; he herded her away from the children before she scared them, took over when she lectured the late returners, and quieten her with her favorite coffee when she talked of the "library crumbling on its periodicals" when she retired.

Until, those in the council not only cut the opening times to three days a week but also Mum's job.

A week after I had come home from hospital, Steven walked in and sighed. "They're getting rid of Beatrice."

"Mum?" I said.

"What are we going to do?" said Steven. "Your Mum is unbearable as it is."

Every morning she burst into the room, startling Baby Bea mid-feed. One breast would be empty and the other still dribbling as Mum would scoop her from me with a "here, let me help—you take a rest."

Twenty minutes later, after several burps, Baby Bea was starving and my huge breast felt like it was bursting.

Steven told me to lock the door, and when I told him that Mum had a key, he offered to change the lock.

It seemed that as soon as Mum was mobile, she just had to see Baby Bea, and before I had time to slip my nipple under its cover, she was practicing her latest story on Baby Bea—until hunger hit, and then it was . . .

"Is she hungry?"

"Do you want me to feed her?"

"Thought you had a dairy in those breasts of yours."

I looked at Steven. "How did they manage it?"

"What?" said Steven.

"Getting rid of her?"

"With a letter."

"She'll be devastated. We can't leave now—can we?"

"She didn't seem to take it too badly," muttered Steven.

"Oh? Was she silent?"

"Yes."

"Shit! A silent mum . . . the worst is yet to come." I sighed. "Better go and see if she's okay or circling the kitchen in a temper."

Beatrice wasn't circling the kitchen; she was staring out the window watching me walk up the path. I waved at her as she looked down. She didn't look miserable at all, let alone angry, just sort of weird. She lifted a mug, gesturing a "coffee?" I, confused, nodded.

"Who needs the library?" she said.

I looked at her. "You love the library—you said it would collapse without you."

"Did I?" she muttered, drying a mug with unconvincing intensity.

"'I am as necessary as a drain to a toilet,' that's what you said."

I looked at George entering the room. "You heard about the library then?" he said.

Mum pulled an *as if I care* face. She looked at me.

"Now I have time to clear things out properly when you leave."

"Leave?" I said.

I looked at her blank face. She was being all cryptic again.

"We are still looking," I said.

"Steven said you found a place," said Mum.

"Well, sort of . . ."

"That's not what he said," said George.

Panic hit my throat . . .

Steven and I had spent months looking for another place to live. Now at home with a baby, he was more determined than ever and had found a home we could afford.

He loved it. I wasn't too keen.

Most of the houses we looked at were old and damp, but this was completely new inside. I should have been jumping for joy. The kitchen hadn't been used, the lounge room was like a hotel reception, the bathroom had a Jacuzzi, and there was a hot tub outside . . . it was enormous.

The sort of house that took all day to tidy . . .

In the sort of place that was in the middle of nowhere and took an hour to get to, most of which was up a single dirt road. It did have incredible views of the loch at the front, but at the back lurked a dark, creaking forest, and there was not a neighbor in sight.

I had never been alone before. I had always been surrounded by shops and noisy neighbors, the sort that bang on the wall if you make too much noise.

This house was isolated—miles from anywhere with no way out but a car, somehow, despite Steven's "What more would you want?"

I wasn't sure.

"No, no, you should go," said Mum. "We all have to move on, don't we, George?"

George threw her a queer look.

"Well . . . yes."

She eyed me. "Don't let me stop you."

"What about Baby Bea?" I stuttered.

"I can still see her," she muttered.

George patted her shoulder.

"It's on the way to my folks'." George laughed. "We'll be passing all the time."

Mum pushed the over-polished mug into the cupboard and, with a sigh, picked up another.

"George says you need space," she muttered, sliding the tea towel around another mug. "Perhaps he's right."

I was about to ask if she was okay, if she'd been at the whisky, when in walked Helen.

"That's the boiler sorted," she said, looking annoyingly at home.

She glanced at me with an uncomfortable smile as George offered her coffee and food. I wondered what else she had been sorting for my mother and why I hadn't been asked.

"What was wrong with the boiler?" I muttered.

"Just a bit of tweaking." Helen smiled.

"Tweaking?"

"Well yes," sniffed Beatrice, "but you've a baby to see to." She smiled at Helen. "Let someone else tweak for a while."

"It was just a small job," said Helen.

"Nothing small with that boiler," I said.

"Didn't mean to interfere," said Helen.

I looked at Mum. "Just because I have a baby doesn't mean . . . I can't do things . . ."

I suddenly felt like crying. I felt replaced, like an old battery.

"I know, but you're just home and, well, a bit emotional," said Mum.

"Me, emotional! What do you mean emotional?" Tears welled in my eyes.

"Forget I said anything," said Mum.

"I can still hold a screwdriver," I sniffed.

"We all know you can," said George, "but you need some rest; how about a coffee and . . . chocolate biscuits?"

I looked at the three of them—cozy, George posing with a packet of Tunnock's Teacakes.

For a moment, I wanted to slap *all of them* senseless, including George.

"No thanks," I huffed. "I think I'll go home, I've packing to do."

Chapter Nine

HOME

A fresh start is over quicker than a sunrise.

We moved a few weeks later.

The thought of moving so soon after having a baby didn't thrill me, but Steven was ecstatic. I guess he was fed up with Mum bounding in unannounced and obsessing about Baby Bea.

Helen, George, and friends from the belly dancing class helped, including my teacher Nefertiti, or "Neff," as we all called her.

Mum watched us empty the bedsit from the window.

I thought she would put up a fight, but she didn't. Instead, she, who hates cooking, packed a snack for all and arrived late in the day when the house was full of boxes.

It was already dark by the time she wheeled herself in, and as she dumped her sandwiches and whisky on the kitchen table, I looked out the window at the forest.

The dark shadows of trees whistled in the wind . . .

We were sitting around the kitchen table chomping into cheese and pickle sandwiches, apart from Mum circling in her wheelchair, when a lull fell on the group. Mum looked across at me and muttered, "This house has a bad vibe."

"Vibe?" Steven looked at me.

"It's full of boxes," said George. "How can there be a vibe?"

With a sniff, Mum handed me a lukewarm dram. "Yes, it's haunted," she said.

The knob on the curtain rail clattered to the ground.

No one said anything.

Steven picked up the knob.

"That's why it was sold so cheap," said Mum.

"They sold it cheap because someone died," said Neff.

The hot tub burst into life under its cover. Mum looked about with an *I told you so* look. "Try telling that to the ghost," she sniffed.

"I switched it on," muttered Steven.

"One guest was seen screaming from the house about a headless chicken," said Mum, "and . . . a headless man with the chicken's head in his hand."

I caught my reflection in the large kitchen window. Behind it blew the trees, creating shadows, creaking and groaning . . . like in a Stephen King movie.

Neff and the others began to clear up, sensing a Beatrice tale a mile long. Neff slid some mugs into the dishwasher as Mum, ignoring the clear-up, continued on about the "mysterious crowing of an invisible chicken."

Neff grabbed Mum's unfinished glass. "I'd give half my scarf collection to stay here," she said.

"You might have to. Sheryl's not keen on chickens, especially ones that have a man's head in its beak."

Mum looked from one face to the other.

"A chicken with a man's head in its beak?" said Neff. She slammed the dishwasher shut. "Must have been a big chicken."

"Definitely," said Mum.

"Aye right," said Steven, "you should keep those stories for the library."

Mum continued talking about the woman who burst into a "Kentucky fried screaming . . . like something from a Stephen King film."

Even I didn't believe that one, but the image followed me to bed that night and for the next week.

❄

A few hours later, my breast aching to feed, I headed into Baby Bea's room and found Mum cuddling her, her face soft and sad.

As soon as Mum saw me, she handed Baby Bea to me.

I looked down at my daughter as I began to feed her, wondering when all this "love" so many mothers spoke about was going to come.

I didn't hear Helen enter until Mum asked her when she was moving in.

I stopped.

Helen blushed. "I haven't said yes yet," she said.

"Come on, it will be way better than that caravan," said Mum. "You know it makes sense."

I looked at Helen. "You've just put a porch on your caravan."

"It leaks," said Mum.

"I haven't even unpacked my kettle and you've got someone else moving in?" I said.

"You have so unpacked your kettle," she said with a tilt of her mug. "What's this I'm drinking, Iron-Bru?"

"It was a figure of speech, Mum," I said, tucking a sleeping Baby Bea back into her bed.

"You have been harping on about moving for months now," said Mum.

"I know but . . . well . . ."

"I haven't said yes yet," interrupted Helen.

Mum looked at Helen. "You can store all your tools below."

Helen coughed and, with a "let's talk about this outside," attempted to steer my Mum away.

I guess I should have been pleased. I'd gotten what I wanted—away from Mum and her interfering—and yet somehow, it made me cry.

But then everything made me cry, and crying made me angry.

I wiped a tear as George and Steven entered. They filled the room with their talk and laughter; I felt like I was suffocating with tears.

I must have looked miserable, because they soon stopped. Mum even gave me one of her annoying *it'll be okay* pats . . .

"It's just your hormones," she said.

Steven said I was tired, which helped about as much as a mobile without a signal. In fact, it enraged me as much as a mobile without a signal, until George chipped in with a "cheer up, it may never happen". . . and another friggin' pat.

I would have bitten his arm off if it wasn't illegal.

"Come on," said Helen, thoughtfully ushering everyone outside.

She was always friggin' thoughtful.

When Helen visited me in the hospital, she took a quick scan of my tearful face and, without one mention of Baby Bea, talked about the next job. The others in the ward looked at her like she was from another planet, pulling faces as she talked of plumbing.

Helen hardly noticed. Instead, as the room filled with visitors cooing over the babies, Helen spread a set of plans onto the bedside table.

"The kitchen's a nightmare," she said, holding the corners of the plans with mugs.

Focusing on the drawings, I wiped my tears, sipped my tea, and nodded. "There is a way around it."

"I knew you would know what to do," said Helen.

I knew what she was doing, and she knew I knew what she was doing . . . and it worked, until the nurse walked in.

"Is that laminated?" she snapped.

The room fell silent.

"Because if it isn't, it's going into the bin. Christ knows how many germs that's carrying—probably enough to contaminate half of Africa."

I watched them all leave Baby Bea's bedroom. The trees rustled outside, Baby Bea's soft breathing filled the room, and I had never felt more alone . . . until I heard George laugh from the kitchen.

"Headless chicken? Not your best story."

I wanted to punch someone in the face.

Chapter Ten

REDUNDANCY

A new beginning often leads to the "same old" ending.

When Mum received her redundancy money, she installed a wet room with piped music, claiming that the only thing better than a hot shower was a hot shower to Jimmy Shan blaring.

George didn't argue.

Instead, he encouraged her to explore her other talents, and when she saw a storyteller in the library, inspiration hit her. She watched a thin Dutch man telling stories of goblins and mice and declared she had "found her calling" and would "just need a lift to the library."

Mum began searching through books for stories, embellishing where she saw fit. Finally, inspired by Halloween, she came up with a pumpkin that refused to be cut, grew legs after midnight, and ran from the kitchen . . . along with her standard spiders, wasps, crocodiles, and vampires.

She had always liked a bit of blood and gore . . .

My mum could make a chocolate cake recipe scary; she had a Bette Davis look that could silence a football hooligan.

When I was a child, a hiccup was enough to get that glare and send you into a spasm of gulping; that could make you sick. The idea of her reading to children was as believable as Steven wanting to drive (until of course I fell pregnant). The only thing she liked doing with children was scaring them, poking her tongue out at them, and shouting ridiculous truths at them, such as "If you eat that, your head will turn inside out."

It wasn't the first time she'd put a child off their ice cream.

She asked me to take her to her first "gig." Apparently, George was doing something hospital-y with his sister and Helen was busy—something about a wedding and her daughter.

I dropped her with a *call me if there are any problems* look at Steven and left her rifling through books waiting for a child to arrive.

I came back to find Mum surrounded by children hanging on her every word—almost wetting themselves with fear as she talked of blood and vampires, on a par with a Hammer horror film.

And she seemed to be enjoying it.

"You will have heard of Count Dracula?" said Mum.

"I have," shouted a red-haired boy.

Beatrice pulled a spooky face. "He sucks blood."

Silence . . .

"He's not real," shouted the red-haired boy.

"From little boys."

"He does not . . ."

"With red hair."

"Mummy?"

"How much blood?" shouted a girl.

"This much," said Mum, doing a large arms-apart measurement. "Sucking until there is no blood left."

The girl's face went white. "Dad! Is that all my blood?"

"He drinks it like Coke," said Mum.

The little girl looked at her father. "Is that true?"

"No, darling, just a story—bit of fun." The father glared at Mum.

"Coke is bad for you," said the red-haired boy.

"Better than having your blood sucked," said Mum.

"Daddy . . ."

"He is the stuff of legends, living forever in the shadows looking for boys, girls, and puppies," said Mum.

"That's enough with the blood," muttered the father.

"Not to mention kittens," whispered Mum.

"I fell over once and got a cut here and here," said another boy.

"You want to be careful, germs will get into that and spread down to your toes and a doctor will cut them off."

"All my toes?"

"And your foot."

"Daddy!"

"Just a story," said the father, "from a silly lady."

"Perhaps, Beatrice, you could stick to the book?" said Steven.

Mum looked at the cartoon book with a "pfff!"

She shut it, bent close to the children, and whispered, "Until the pumpkin with legs came along."

"Pumpkin?"

"Yes, the pumpkin had legs so long he could step over fences."

The children hushed, silent, as she told three stories of a pumpkin faster than a speeding bullet and more likeable than Anna and Elsa in *Frozen*. And when Mum, with great animation, told how the pumpkin smashed the vampire into a pile of spaghetti bolognaise full of garlic, the children's faces lit up, some squealed with delight.

"Go pumpkin go!"

"Tell me more!"

I was shocked. My mum hated cooking; she didn't even know how to boil spaghetti, let alone chop garlic.

She moved onto stories of dragons, goblins, and cars that ran over rats that tried to eat the pumpkin, who was now called Legs.

I had no idea that my mum could be so entertaining, let alone so imaginative. As far as I knew, the only thing she ever read was the sports page of the *Herald*, and there she was telling stories like Scotland's answer to Roald Dahl. My mum was unrecognizable with children; she captivated them.

As I drove Mum home, I struggled not to praise her. Mum likes to crow about things, making you regret any compliment, but before I had a chance to say "Well done," Mum started to talk of Helen, and any possible compliment vanished.

As she talked, I silently huffed. I wanted to scream, "Well, get *her* to friggin' pick you up then." I didn't; instead, I stupidly listened to her, my anger festering.

"That woman is a dream," she said. "An absolute dream."

"Glad to hear it, Mum."

"She's a wizard with a hammer, not to mention a drill."

"I *have* worked with her," I muttered.

"Give her a set of plans and a mastic gun and she'll transform anything—you name it."

"I get the picture," I said with a sharp wrench of a gear.

"She has patience I have never seen before—more angel than woman." She turned to me. "We have coffee together every day."

"Aye, very good." I pulled into the driveway.

"She confides in me."

"Won't last."

"What?" said Mum.

"I said very good."

"You know, her daughter is getting married," said Mum.

I stopped the car and walked around to the boot. I had no idea but didn't want to give Mum something else to crow about.

"I was the first to know," she yelled to the back of the car. "Did she not tell you?"

"We used to work together, Mum, doesn't mean we're bosom buddies."

I pulled Mum's wheelchair from the boot and wheeled it to her side.

"Steven knows."

"Steven?" I stopped, wrenching the brakes on with a yank. "He is her brother," I snapped.

"And George," said Mum, shuffling across her seat.

"Every man and his dog have been told then," I muttered.

"What was that?"

"I said George has a kind face."

"The postwoman hasn't, she's got a face like a smoked sausage and she knows. You sure Helen didn't tell you?"

"No, Mum, I think I would have remembered a friggin' wedding."

"Well, it's just that you're not yourself lately. Forgetting things, bit snappy."

"Snappy? Who says I'm snappy?"

"And tearful," said Mum. "Folk are kind of . . ."

"What?"

"Well they don't like to upset you. Maybe Helen thought . . ."

"Not telling me would cheer me up?"

"Sheryl," said Mum, "stop being so . . . so . . . touchy."

I exploded, right there in the driveway. I snapped.

"Wouldn't you be if your bits had been wrenched open like a car boot and then packed back like a toddler shoves his stuffed toys?"

"Sheryl, I hardly think your bits have been shoved back in; they weren't out in the first place."

"What would you know?" I yelled.

I watched Mum wheel herself back to her home. She stopped at the door and turned to look at me.

"Sheryl, you had a baby, not a major operation."

"Mass destruction of my fanny," I yelled.

"Don't exaggerate."

"When they catheterized me, I swore like a banshee . . ."

"Steven told me."

"Told you?"

"Yes, he said he never heard anything like it," said Mum.

I followed her inside.

"I was told it was an uncomplicated birth," said Mum. "As smooth as butter, so that Polish doctor said." She sighed. "Nice man."

"Arsehole," I snapped, removing her shoes.

"What was that?"

"I said that's not what I remember, I remember Steven holding my hand while the 'nice Polish doctor' stitched up my ripped birth canal while talking about his camping trip to a young nurse like it was chat-up central."

Mum pulled a face.

"They told me to relax," I said to Mum. "Bit hard when your bits are being laced up like a boot while you're listening to the joys of a pop-up tent."

"Well, it's all over now, dear," said Mum.

"That's what Steven says."

I followed Mum into the kitchen and watched as she wheeled about, completing her arrival routine of jacket off, phone in holder, radio on. She asked if it wasn't time for me to go home to feed Baby Bea; despite the small leakage, I said no. The truth was, I didn't want to go home. I was as down as a Leonard Cohen song, and Steven being annoyingly chipper didn't help.

Mum flicked the kettle on. She eyed me, her face softening.

"The best thing about having a baby is the toast and tea." She laughed. "Almost as satisfying as sex."

"Yes, and just like sex, the second helping is usually a bit shit," I said.

Chapter Eleven

AMY

Anger has its place, just not near a hammer.

I left Mum's with my breast screaming for a decent milking and headed for the car. What had I become? I never smiled, let alone laughed. I hardly recognized myself; it was like I was possessed by some madwoman. No wonder Helen didn't tell me anything. I probably would have either ripped her face off, burst into tears, or maybe even both . . .

Helen was in the garage with her daughter, Amy.

Helen, emptying the van of tools, handed a few at a time to Amy, who dumped them on the garage floor in a temper.

I was just about to make an "Isn't my mum annoying?" comment when I noticed they sounded pissed off. Then I heard the sort of conversation you really didn't want to hear and yet couldn't move away from in case you missed a bit, and Helen was swearing.

A drill crashed to the ground.

"Will you stop saying 'fuck,' Mum? It doesn't sound right."

"Well, what do you expect?" said Helen. She jumped out of the van. Amy stopped with a glare.

"Expect? I was just telling you about our wedding."

Helen paused, then looked at the tools scattered about the floor with a shake of her head. "Fucking hell . . . why didn't you pile them into boxes as we went?" she said, uselessly shifting boxes about. "Way fucking easier."

"It's my wedding," said Amy.

"So you keep saying."

"And he's my dad, for Christsake," said Amy.

Helen stopped. "I am not asking you to understand, but at least show some tact."

Amy huffed.

"How would you feel?" said Helen.

"Mum, I am getting married. His name is bound to crop up."

I bent to help Helen. She didn't seem to notice.

"If your man treated you like I was treated . . ." She wiped her eyes.

"I said I don't want to hear this." Amy turned to me. "She doesn't want me talking about Dad." She glared at her mother. "She doesn't even want him at the wedding."

"I never said that. Just . . . well . . . why is he walking you down the aisle?"

"He's my father?"

"He never looked after you."

"Mum."

"Wouldn't even have a coffee with us," said Helen, stuffing tools into the wrong box like they were to blame. "Too fucking busy."

The box, overflowing, toppled. I made a grab to stop it and missed.

"Fuck! Fuck! Fuck!" said Helen. "Now look what you made me do."

"I'll get it," I shouted.

"Stop saying 'fuck,'" said Amy.

"Smashed up *my* stuff . . ." She stopped, trying to compose herself.

I lifted a hammer from her hand.

She looked at me. "He drove a tractor over my plants."

"Mum, he hasn't driven a tractor in years."

"I spent hours in that garden and he fucking drove a tractor over it like it was a pile of shit."

Amy looked at me.

"That was years ago, Mum."

"Every Saturday night he'd go somewhere."

"Come on, Mum."

"Like his so-called aunt's, and did they invite me? I may as well have had *fucking* rabies."

"I don't remember that," said Amy.

"I hid it from you. I wanted you to be happy."

"His aunt *is* a bit of a cow," I muttered.

Helen shoved a box on top of another; they tumbled to the ground. "Fuck."

"You're making something out of nothing," said Amy.

Helen stopped. "Something out of nothing?"

"Yes."

"Well, is this nothing?" She kicked the boxes across the room.

"Now you're being childish," snapped Amy, and with an "unbelievable," she headed for the car.

Helen, still steaming, looked at me.

"All these years I tried to be a good mother and for what? For *anal features* to give her away at her wedding?"

She blew hard on her nose.

"While I'm sitting in the back like a lampshade without a friggin' bulb." She looked at me. "So unfair."

I stared at the mess in the garage. The last person I expected to see lose it, let alone swearing like a hooligan with Tourette's, was Helen. She always seemed indestructibly, cool.

I mean, this was a woman who coped with second-hand washing machines and rats that didn't take no for an answer, who had taught herself to mend things. Who was as familiar with a hammer as a hairdryer, a legend with a drill, and a demon with a chainsaw. She paraded about on roofs like she was on a catwalk.

I looked at her. "Shall I pick up some boxes?"

She didn't argue. Instead, she burst into tears.

I was taken aback. Helen crying? I hardly knew her, and she was blubbering in front of me like I could help.

What do I say?

"It's a wedding," I came up with. "Everyone gets emotional."

"I just thought we'd bond, have a mother-and-daughter moment." She looked at me. "Not anymore. He gives up the fags and booze and suddenly he is a fucking hero, and my arse is out the window. We have as much chance of bonding as you and fucking Beatrice."

"Shall I call Steven?" I said.

She wiped her eyes, blew her nose, and looked at me.

"When I first married Henry, he was so busy I never saw him," she said. "He promised." She sighed. "Nothing changed; he was never there, and that house—Jesus."

She started to cry again.

"The doors never locked, the cupboards have no shelves, the carpets are from someone's attic. Everything came from someone's fucking attic, and there was always a set of tools somewhere to trip over."

She kicked a box.

"My toenails are a mess, thanks to his fucking drills—the times I stubbed my toes on them."

"You sure you don't want Steven?" I muttered.

"I put up with it all. I thought it would get better, that one day he would maybe just once—fucking once—spend an hour with me, a few minutes, share a joke."

She shook her head.

I patted her back, and when that was not enough, I wrapped an arm around her shoulder which set her off again . . . crying like someone close had died.

She blew her nose.

"I tried to fix a door once," she cried. "He put his fist through it. He put his fist through a lot of things, anything I sorted, until I stopped . . . fixing . . . caring."

"There, there," I tapped her back. "You're not with him anymore, you needn't worry . . ."

"He was always someone else's mate, making me look like a fool, and now he's fucking Amy's mate. She thinks he's great, if only she—they—anyone knew."

"Not everyone thinks he's great," I muttered.

❋

That night, as I lay in bed waiting for Steven, I stared at the ceiling.

Steven was cleaning his teeth in an annoyingly loud way, loud enough to wake Baby Bea, and I told him so.

He didn't say anything. Instead, he made what seemed an extra-loud gurgle-and-spit noise.

I had spent the night telling Steven about Helen's over-the-top reaction, ending with a "she left him years ago, so why now" comment, and for some reason, he seemed pissed in a nonspeaking way, and his whole teeth-cleaning routine was just rubbing it in.

Steven never used to spit; he used to quietly dribble, like he didn't want to spoil the moment. His getting-to-bed routine was a pleasure to behold, ending with a flick of the light and a quirky comment about giving me something to dream about. Now he was giving big "old git" gurgles like something out of an old folks' home . . .

Finally, after what seemed the polishing of the Sistine Chapel, he, after a robust cough, appeared, pyjamas annoyingly tight about his slim waist.

"You have no idea what that poor cow has been through," he snapped, and then, with a dismissive flick of the duvet, he slid into his side of the bed and huffed his back to me.

I waited to hear his snore, but all I heard was another huff, followed by a punch of the pillow.

"This is your flaming pillow," he said.

"No it's not," I said without really knowing.

"Yes it is; where's mine?" he snapped.

"Here." I tossed my pillow at him, setting off an argument about bed making until Baby Bea woke with a cry.

Chapter Twelve

SHEEP

Apologies are often hidden.

Normally, Steven's bad moods lasted as long as a TV ad, but since the move and my descent into a black hole, Steven seemed to have lost his patience.

As I appeared at the breakfast table, he greeted me with a nod and a look I cringed from.

Is it the lack of sex that's making things so bad, or has the magic truly gone?

Steven placed his crust onto his plate and, without looking at me, flicked on the kettle.

"Coffee?" he said.

I nodded. With great precision, Steven poured himself one, lifted a week-old newspaper, and nestled back into his chair.

My mug was still empty.

Steven often talked of his sister. They were close, but I never saw much of her while she was married, and while Steven had all the sympathy in the world for her, I felt jealous, along with every other lousy feeling.

Steven, lingering over his coffee with slurps on a par with his tooth-brushing, flicked open the paper and began to read like he hadn't read it before.

I poured my own coffee.

"All right," I said, "I am sorry."

"Are you though?"

"It's just that . . . well . . . it's a bit hard coping with this new *wrist-slitting* Helen. I mean, she *has* moved into our place."

"A godsend," muttered Steven, still supposedly engrossed in the paper.

"Taken over my mother."

"Another godsend." He slurped.

"And here I am with nipples the size of oranges."

"Another godsend." He caught my eye. "Well . . . maybe not."

"I mean, she's fallen on her feet; all's well, Mum thinks she's the tits, George not far behind. She's not the one with a garage for a fanny."

"I wouldn't know, haven't seen it," said Steven with a flick of a page.

"So why now, after all this time?" I said.

Steven began to talk about suppressed anger, survival, and squeezing pimples, which had me totally confused, until he threw "Donna" into the mix.

I stared out onto our garden. "Forgot about that, it was so long ago."

"Exactly," muttered Steven with another page flick.

"Amy was about ten and talking of being a vet."

"Exactly. She thought it was great," said Steven.

"Everyone thought it was great, apart from Helen," I muttered.

It was a rare night in the pub with Steven, Henry, and his crowd. Henry had spent a fair bit of it talking about Donna, who was "almost part of the family." She sounded like a friend, a long-distance cousin, and his crowd, who thought everything was funny after a skinful, wanted to meet her. Even I did.

Henry, with a "Helen will love it" promise, took us all back to his home. None of us thought about Helen.

Henry, drunk to the point of needing a hand up the steps, motioned us all to go in, making so much noise that the neighbor's dog woke up.

Amy, who was looking after the neighboring farmer's pet sheep, had just come back from a late-night "making sure all is well" visit. She looked cute in her wellies over her pyjamas and happily followed her father to get Donna, while we made ourselves at home in the lounge room.

It was Christmastime, and Helen had not long finished putting up the cards. There were presents under the tree and fairy lights blinking.

We all basked by the fire as Helen went to get us drinks. Donna was meant to be a surprise . . .

Twenty minutes later, Henry appeared at the door. "Heeeeere's Donna," he shouted like a game show host, throwing open the door to a full-blown sheep looking terrified.

She skidded into the room and began manically circling for a way out, leaving a trail of black poo pellets behind her.

Everyone thought it was funny except Helen, who, appearing with a tray of drinks, shouted, "Get *it* out, I just cleaned!"

"Come on Mum, he's cute," laughed Amy.

"Yeah, come on, Mum," laughed another.

"Just because that sheep has a name doesn't mean it's house-trained," said Helen, sending everyone into hysterics.

Donna skidded on her pee.

"She's pissing everywhere—get her out of here," shouted Helen.

"It's only piss," shouted someone.

Steven tried to catch Donna, sending her into a frenzy, crushing presents and knocking the coal bucket over. A few cards fell; Donna skidded on one, "Jingle Bells" began to play, and everyone started to sing along.

Me, I am ashamed to say, included.

Helen picked up the card. "For fuck's sake."

Henry called her a wet blanket and more, sending us all into more laughter . . . until finally the tree crashed to the ground, right on top of the coal.

Donna skidded, smearing coal everywhere.

This time, no one laughed, as Steven, with the help of Amy, managed to remove Donna.

"I wonder how long it took her to clean up the mess," I said.

"Not as long as you would think," said Steven, "but it was her last Christmas tree."

"Forgot about that too," I said.

"She put up with it all because she didn't know how she could bring up Amy on her own," said Steven. "Now she's trying to come to terms with what she suppressed for years. That anger's got to come out sometime, like pus from a pimple."

Finally, the pimple makes sense.

I looked at Steven. "I guess that's why you're a writer and I'm a builder . . ."

Chapter Thirteen

SEAGULLS

There is more than one way to peel a pumpkin.

Within a month of moving into the new home, Neff had arranged for the belly dance girls to celebrate with a hot tub party, along with the Bag Lady, who camped in Neff's garden, and her friend Betty.

Steven was to spend the night away, while I was "not to do anything but allow myself to be pampered."

I asked Helen to join, as she needed "cheering up."

She had just been to her daughter's hen do and was still recovering. Henry, being generous, had paid for the weekend, and Helen was fed up hearing about it.

A bonfire was set up near the dark shadows of the trees, which rustled a noise that had me regretting listening to Mum's latest headless chicken story.

Mum turned up in the early afternoon, along with George and an armful of vegetables for barbecuing—including pumpkins. Mum proceeded to talk about her latest story and the house's so-called "vibe," while George, spying log cutting, went outside.

When I say *talking*, it was to Baby Bea rather than me. As soon as Mum saw Baby Bea, she dropped her bag of vegetables and scooped her up.

"Don't you worry about this place," she whispered to Baby Bea. "I brought pumpkins to protect you."

Potatoes rolled from the bag, followed by a cabbage. I bent to pick them up, idly wondering what a cabbage had to do with a barbecue, when I caught sight of Mum twirling Baby Bea with a high-as-a-kite smile.

"How about a hello, Mum?" I said.

I was still in my pyjamas, and she hadn't even noticed.

"It's a given," she said, followed by enough cooing to put a lion to sleep.

Baby Bea was as mesmerized as Mum; I may as well have been a chopping board for all they cared. I looked at the two of them.

"I am still here," I said.

Mum didn't hear but took Baby Bea out onto the back porch and started telling her where great pumpkins hid at night. She didn't even bat an eyelid when she saw Neff and the Bag Lady organizing things, let alone George acting the goat with a couple of logs.

Mum and Neff gel like oil and water. They tolerate each other like politicians of opposing parties, and Mum hated it when Neff and George "carried on." I was expecting a stiff nod from Mum followed by an "is it absolutely necessary for them to be here at the crack of dawn?" comment. Instead, Mum laughed and waved with Baby Bea's hand.

"Look at Uncle George. Isn't he silly?" she said.

I give up, I thought and headed for the bedroom.

I figured three visitors warranted more than pyjamas; besides, Steven would be home soon for lunch.

"Are you feeding her properly?" Mum shouted at me.

"Of course, but you keep interrupting," I shouted, tugging at the knots in my hair.

"She feels light. Doesn't she feel light to you?" shouted Mum.

"It's natural," I yelled, "they lose a bit in the first week."

"A bit? Who said that? I don't remember you or Lindsey losing a bit."

I appeared at the kitchen. Mum, with a sarcastic *going out then?* look, eyed my pulled-together outfit: leggings, a large T-shirt, and an even larger cardigan. Normally, she would have said it and more; instead, she turned back to my daughter and jiggled her little finger.

"Would you like me to treat you to a haircut?" she said without looking up.

"I am growing it," I snapped, slapping the kettle on. "Steven says long hair suits me."

"Hmmm . . . he would, wouldn't he, *Baby-darling Bee?*"

Baby Bea started to doze.

Mum put her in her cot with an exaggerated "she's light" jostle.

"Are you sure she's eating enough?" she said.

"Steven says she's fine," I said.

"What would he know?"

"As much as you."

"Yes, but I have been there and got the T-shirt," said Mum. "He's still looking at T-shirts."

"That was years ago," I said. "And even then, *you* didn't look after Lindsey . . ."

I stopped. Mum, oblivious yet again, was tucking a blanket about my sleeping daughter.

She looked about the kitchen, wheeled herself to the sink, and began to uselessly pile dishes. I told her to leave it, but she didn't hear. Instead, she began to ask where things were while cleaning things in that annoying "you're not managing" sort of way.

"Oh, I nearly forgot," she muttered, tossing a grey cloth at the bin like it was a dead rat. "Steven asked me to remind you he wasn't coming home for lunch; any more dishcloths?"

"Oh," I said.

"I don't think there's enough time in his lunch break to come here and back." She eyed my long face and mumbled a patronizing "dear," followed by an even more patronizing pat.

"Probably," I muttered.

Mum asked me if I was "sleeping okay," and before I had a chance to say, "not really," she launched into stories of the "invisible" neighbours with an "I found out more" while endlessly polishing a surface.

The last thing I wanted was one of Mum's scare-the-crap-out-of-me stories. "If it's bad, I don't want to hear it," I said. "It's hard enough waking up to feed without scary stories to keep me awake."

Mum muttered a "very good, dear" as she moved on to buttering toast with an intensity very unlike her.

Neff and the Bag Lady entered.

Mum pushed some toast towards them with a smile and a flick of imaginary crumbs.

"Coffee?" Mum said like a top-class waitress.

Neff threw me a *what's with her?* look. (Mum was not the waitress type.)

I shrugged as the Bag Lady slid a crust into her mouth with a "hmmm."

Mum moved on to uselessly mopping a wet rag about the bench as she talked of how the place next door has been on the market for so long they've made it a holiday home.

"Something to do with the ice cream wars," she said with a flick of the chopping board.

"Ice cream wars? That was centuries ago," said the Bag Lady.

"And the place *next door* is miles from here," said Neff.

Somehow, the thought of being miles from any neighbor seemed worse than living next door to criminals.

Mum looked at me, and her face softened as she patted my cheek. "But I am sure it's nothing to worry about." She looked about the mess in the kitchen.

"They have an amazing cleaner," she said, then stopped as she saw Helen appear in the garden, walking about the trees.

Mum stared into the garden, her eyes glued to Helen. There was something on her mind, and waiting for it was doing my head in.

I was about to ask when she said, "Does Helen come here much?"

My mind flitted back to the garage and the excessive use of the word *fuck*.

"Helen?" I muttered.

"Yes, her out there, walking around the trees. What *is* she doing?"

"I think she is making a plan. I've asked her to cut them down."

Mum nearly choked on her tea. "Trees?

I nodded.

"You told Steven?"

"He's cool with it."

"Cool? Doesn't he love them?"

And before I had a chance to answer, Mum began to tut about Helen and how "that girl had changed."

Helen, giving into Mum had moved into my old bedsit and Mum had bequeathed her my DIY list, until Helen was last seen tossing slates like a madwoman.

"Helen was the sort of person who smiled in the face of adversity. Now she just throws things," muttered Mum. "The other day I was in the middle of tucking into a scone when I looked out the window and there she was like a wild woman up the ladder. I've never seen anyone clean gutters like that before. She was literally ripping lumps of moss and lobbing them at a seagull. What's a poor seagull done to deserve that?"

Silence . . .

"And since when did she start friggin' swearing?"

Neff and I looked at each other. This from a woman who swears at the drop of a scone?

"She had seen the ex," said Mum.

"That'll do it," I muttered.

"Yes, it seems she was passing the loch and there he was tossing crusts at a passing duck—laughing with Amy. Apparently, that was enough to turn her into a gull-killing Frankenstein."

George entered. "The gull survived."

"Yes, but the gutters didn't." Mum looked at me. "I think she's gone mad."

Baby Bea began to cry, and Mum moved to pick her up.

"I wouldn't leave her near a TV remote, let alone a baby," she said.

I hadn't told anyone about the garage incident and never spoke of it to Helen either, despite the fact that I saw her most days.

She normally popped in after work to skull several teas, raid my biscuit stash, or rummage through my fridge for leftovers. In fact, I was beginning to wonder if the only place she ate was at my home.

She didn't even look at Baby Bea or ask after Steven, and she never talked of her daughter's wedding. Instead, she would chat like a work-man, through slurps of tea, about work.

She was the only one who didn't comment about the state of my house. In fact, she didn't seem to care, trudging into the kitchen in her work boots and slinging a dirty cup under the tap with a "you want one?"

"Shh, don't say anything, here she comes," muttered Mum.

"We'll be late," said George.

"I said shh . . ." Mum hissed.

"The folks are cooking for us," said George.

"Folks?"

"My folks," said George, "remember? My sister?"

Mum looked at me as Helen walked in.

"I don't think I'll make it tonight," she said. "I'm off to help Amy choose a dress."

"Oh," said Mum. "A sort of mother-and-daughter thing."

"Yes," she said, looking pleased with herself.

"Let's hope there are no seagulls," muttered Mum.

Chapter Fourteen

GIRLS' NIGHT OUT

Sexy is as sexy does.

Helen did come after all, very late and distressed. She had been held up at the police station for verbally abusing a parking attendant.

We were sitting about the campfire at the time: Neff, the Bag Lady, her pal Betty, Neff's pal Mavis, and Iona, who had joined the belly dancing troupe when it was all but finished.

Baby Bea had spent the night being passed from one woman to another, each with their own special baby talk. Except for Neff; she didn't do babies.

Instead, she asked me if I was still doing my hip circles and insisted on a show.

"She's breastfeeding," said Mavis. "That's supposed to put things back into order."

"Not like belly dancing," said Neff.

Mavis filled everyone's glass, and as the wine flowed, the women moved on to ideas of making a teepee for Baby Bea like the Bag Lady's in Neff's garden. Not exactly what I had in mind for my wee girl, which I did my best to explain, but no one listened.

The Bag Lady's teepee is decorated in a kaleidoscope of colorful skulls, shells, and other bits of junk collected from her walks with

Betty. Their idea of decorating was as outrageous as a woman living in a teepee well past her pension age.

There was an old bath mat used for a welcome mat, which frequently blew across the garden, and hand-painted junk that tinkled at the slightest breeze. It was not the first time junk had landed in a neighbor's yard after a decent autumn wind, and it was not the first time the neighbor not only returned the junk but added some of their own.

The more the wine flowed, the more outrageous the women's idea of a tent for Baby Bea became. Even Iona, a "horsey" woman, was drawn in.

"We could make clowns," she said.

I choked on my wine. "Clowns? Here?"

"Great idea," shouted Neff.

"Here?" I repeated.

"One could be playing the drums," added Mavis.

I threw her a look. "Steven hates clowns," I lied.

They waved me away with a "pfff . . . he'll love it."

I was about to say more—how much the place scared me at night, and how clowns waving about like something from Stephen King's *It* were the last things I needed—when Baby Bea began to make "I need a feed" noises.

I pulled Baby Bea to my breast, waiting for the initial *ouch!* And felt a pleasant sensation of her warm lips touching my skin . . .

I stopped, waited . . . *No pain?*

Neff threw another log on the fire. The fire roared up on the dry log, playing shadows on Baby Bea's pink skin, and for a moment the women watched.

"Never had a baby," muttered Neff.

"Me neither," said Mavis.

Iona, who had three grown-up children, topped up her drink. "Enjoy it," she said. "Once they grow up, you're lucky if they ring, let alone visit."

I looked down at my daughter drinking like she'd never been fed before. Perhaps that pasty old nurse was right: feeding was a "piece of piss" after all. "Once your nipples adjust," she'd said, "you won't look back."

I closed my eyes and sighed. For the first time in ages (despite pending clowns), I felt a sense of peace, like I could actually make a go of being a mother.

"This is heaven," I muttered.

A few nodded an "I'm glad" as the Bag Lady began to mutter about "earthy things lurking in the forest."

"Don't go in there," I muttered, still looking at Baby Bea's soft face.

The Bag Lady disappeared into the trees with just a flicker of a pen torchlight.

I looked up. "Did she hear?"

"Wouldn't worry," said Neff. "Betty will soon follow."

Betty tutted, pulled a mega-large high-beam torch from her bag, and strode into the forest with a "what's she up to now?"

Neff nudged me as Betty's torch lit up the trees like a stadium, making mysterious shapes that waved in the wind.

There was a rustle . . .

Followed by a shout . . .

"Mind!"

"Mind?"

"That's my toe."

"Is it? Fuck."

Silence . . .

More rustling . . .

We stared into the shadows of the forest as torchlights flickered and flashed.

"Don't shine it there . . . there!"

"Where?"

"I said *there* . . . here, give me that."

"It's my friggin' torch."

Mavis topped our glasses with a "more?"

Betty finally appeared with the Bag Lady behind her rubbing dirt from a skull.

She held it high in the air. "What do you think?" she shouted to the group.

"It's a skull, like all the others," muttered Betty.

"Yes, but painted with smiley faces"—she turned it in her hand—"and glitter. Baby Bea will love it."

"Since when have you done smiley faces?" snapped Betty.

The Bag Lady, with a pleased-with-herself smile, headed inside to wash the skull with Betty behind her shouting, "You can't do that in the sink."

The other women laughed as I withdrew Baby Bea from my breast —limp as a rag doll, zoned out like she was stoned. The women watched as I put her into her basket, then Neff pulled out the Bag Lady's drum.

An hour later, the women were dancing, and I was watching like I had never seen it before.

It seemed a century ago that I danced for the wrestlers.

When I first discovered belly dancing, it was like sex. I wasn't getting any, and hip-circling really soothed the feeling.

Steven still talks of the first time he saw me dance: "the sexiest thing with clothes on," he called it. And it wasn't long before I was giving him private dances; he loved them, cheered me on, even videoed me.

"My foxy goddess," he used to say, along with other delicious things which usually led to wonderful love making.

It seemed a lifetime ago . . .

I hadn't felt anything in ages. My body felt like one of Mum's pumpkins, and as for sex, I'd rather have a tooth pulled.

I watched the others laugh and dance with no intention of joining in. I used to love dancing in front of a spellbound crowd; I couldn't be arsed now. I can't even remember the last time I listened to the Egyptian drums. My bits felt like they had been ripped apart, circling them was the last thing I wanted to do.

I could see Neff working up to pulling me up and Iona stopping her. Then the drumming stopped as Helen walked in.

Chapter Fifteen

THE PARKING ATTENDANT

"I'm sorry" doesn't always cut the mustard.

When Helen arrived, the laughing stopped; she looked anything but happy. Her "going shopping" clothes were splattered with flecks of blood, and she looked like she had been bawling her eyes out.

"You finally made it," said Mavis.

Neff patted a log with a "still warm."

We waited . . .

"Amy is a bit fucked off," she said.

I handed Helen a drink.

"I went mental at a parking attendant."

Silence.

"Forgot about the parking meter."

She stared into the fire . . .

We waited.

She sipped.

"Go on," said Neff.

"It's not nice," muttered Helen.

"Just tell us," said Neff.

Helen drained her glass and talked of her day with Amy like it had happened to someone else, like a scene in a movie.

"We were looking at wedding dresses," she said. "And we almost had a mother-and-daughter moment when Henry phoned with a 'money's no object when it comes to my baby girl' offer."

"That was nice of him," said Mavis.

"That's what Amy said," muttered Helen. She looked at her empty glass.

"But you can't deal with it," said Betty.

"Well, yes."

"It's like it's a competition and, well, you're losing," said Betty.

Helen looked at her. "Yes."

"She's your daughter," said Mavis. "Every daughter loves their mum . . ." She caught my eye and stopped. "Don't they?"

"It's not like I'm loaded," said Helen. "All I can offer is a hug and a listening ear. He's the one who kept the business, the house, and the cat. I don't even have a fucking cat and Amy loves them."

"Cats? What's cats got to do with it?" muttered Mavis.

"My sister went through the same thing," said Betty. "Her husband bribed their children with horses."

"Horses?" said Mavis.

"So what happened next?" said Neff, gesturing to the blood.

"Then I see a podgy parking attendant," said Helen, "with a face like an avalanche. I waved at her, she pretended she didn't see, so I ran to the window. 'I'm just coming out,' I shouted, and do you know what she did?"

"I can guess," muttered Mavis.

"She blanked me—"

"Bloody parking attendants," said Mavis.

"—and pulled out her fucking pad."

Helen, still with a blank face, went on to describe how she tried to reason with a woman who "made Trump look like a fairy godmother."

She sipped.

"Then Henry drove by in his fancy 'I'm a great shag' sports car with a toot *and* a blonde . . . and get this."

"What?"

"*He* offered to help *me*." She looked at us. "'Can I help?' he said."

"What's wrong with that?" said Neff.

Helen, ignoring Neff, carried on. She talked of seeing red, yelling, an embarrassed daughter, and her wrestling a pad from a parking attendant who had the grip of a Rottweiler.

"It gets a bit blurry after that," said Helen, "but I'll never forget the look on Amy's face when the police arrived. 'Mum,' she said."

Helen sighed.

"And?" said Neff.

"Can't remember what else." Helen looked at me. "Apparently the attendant has a black eye."

Helen slumped. "And I called her 'Hitler incarnate.'"

"Jesus wept," muttered Mavis.

"Bit strong," muttered Iona.

Helen stared into the fire.

"Plus, I think I overused the word *fuck*. In fact, I might have told a few to fuck off."

"Bloody hell," said Betty.

"Including a policeman."

"I'm sure he's been told to fuck off plenty of times," said the Bag Lady.

Helen, thanks to a decent policeman, was given a fine, along with mandatory anger management classes. The parking attendant had a record of being assaulted due to her ability to ignore drivers' "I'm just coming out" waves. She, having failed her driver test so many times she had a standing order at the test centre, hated *all* drivers and paced her patch like a sniffer dog on the scent of something illegal.

Some say she had tampered with the meters, which, according to the same "some," was being "looked into."

Helen retreated into her bedsit, refusing any "fancy a spot of lunch?" from Mum. It seems the parking ticket had pushed her over the edge.

Mum suggested I visit and talk about "building and tools" to help "take her mind off things."

Me, help her?

I mean, I was struggling to be a mum, let alone a stay-at-home mum. Baby Bea woke several times during the night and took ages to feed. I was so tired I dropped off as soon as I sat down and burst into tears at anything; even the Simpsons made me blubber. And our new house, which seemed the size of a hotel compared to the old bedsit, seemed impossible to keep tidy. I couldn't remember where I put anything.

I burnt toast, made soft hard-boiled eggs. Steven said little until I tossed a burnt pan at the remains of the bonfire accompanied by a volley of swear words; then he took over not only the cooking but the shopping with a "perhaps we should see a doctor?"

How could I help someone else, especially a woman on the verge of exploding? Whose reasoning was on par with Homer Simpson's?

Mum said it was all those years of bottling it up that had cracked Helen. "Being nice has a price," she said, "when you do it to survive."

Which was rich coming from the same mouth that blasted me on a regular basis about my lack of "mum skills."

I tried to tell my mother that I was busy, that perhaps *she*, being the "font of all knowledge," was probably better placed to help.

Mum, ignoring the "font of all knowledge," arranged a time for me to have some lunch and visit Helen while she could "see to the wee one." Which meant her changing nappies, followed by comments about Baby Bea's imaginary skin conditions and weight loss.

After a lunch of forgettable soup and sandwiches, I ventured across on the pretense of seeing Helen. I was not in the best of trim, as Mum, having spotted a real live rash under Baby Bea's neck, talked with patronizing mummy-ness about the wonders of zinc.

I was feeling the sting of being wrong. I knew there was a pot of zinc in the boot somewhere, and I was on a mission to find it—bugger the whole Helen issue.

As I headed to the car, fantasizing about proving Mum wrong, I heard Amy and Helen talking. The bedsit wasn't exactly soundproof.

Amy was worried about her mother's ability to "ruin her big day," as she was showing signs of paranoia on par with a Russian spy.

In her blind rage during the parking meter incident, Helen had called Henry a middle-aged degenerate hitting on blondes young enough to be his granddaughter. "A sports car is not a penis," she shouted, which had pretty much been the last straw for Amy.

I stopped at my car, opened the boot, and began to rummage as Amy called her mother a moron who "jumped to conclusions that even a moron would be ashamed of."

"That's 'cause nobody tells me anything," said Helen.

"That's 'cause you explode like a landmine," said Amy.

"That's a ridiculous analogy."

"You haven't seen yourself explode," said Amy.

"You haven't lived with your dad," shouted Helen.

"I have too."

"Look," said Helen. "When you see a man in a sports car with a blonde young enough to be his granddaughter—"

"Daughter," snapped Amy. "It is physically impossible for him to have a granddaughter of driving age."

"—who has spent his entire driving life tooting at young women like some boy racer—"

"He never did that with me," said Amy.

"—the last thing you expect is for that blonde to be a salesperson and the sports car to be a possible hire for a wedding."

"Well, I would," said Amy.

"Yes, but you're not married to him."

"Neither are you, which you seem to forget."

"Forget? How can I when you keep talking about him?" yelled Helen.

"Oh, for fuck's sake," shouted Amy, "it's pointless talking to you."

The bedsit door crashed shut.

Footsteps raced down to the garage.

I pulled a box from the boot. The bottom fell open and an avalanche of baby things cluttered to the floor. I pushed the contents about with my foot; no zinc . . .

"Wait!" shouted Helen.

The bedsit door crashed shut again.

Amy stopped at the garage door, catching me trying to squash everything back into a boot that felt the size of a matchbox.

"It's you," said Amy. "Mum thought it was the parking attendant come back to haunt her." She feigned a laugh.

Helen appeared behind her. "That's not true," she muttered.

Amy looked at me. "Tell her she's paranoid."

I stared at them, both standing with the same angry stance. I didn't know what to say. I mean, if I got it wrong, there could be another explosion.

"You haven't any zinc, have you?" I muttered.

"Zinc?" said Helen.

"Just tell her," said Amy, "she listens to you."

"No really, I'm in need of some zinc, and . . ." I stopped. "She listens to me?"

"Yes, of course."

No one listens to me.

Chapter Sixteen

THE LAWYER

Punching a cushion doesn't solve anything.

After Amy left, Helen took me upstairs to her bedsit.

"I've got some zinc," she said and, as I followed, she talked about how everything was so "fucking unfair."

Mum was right, she wasn't handling things well. She hadn't unpacked anything, the floor was a sea of boxes and bin bags, some unopened with tight knots at the top, others spilling out with clothes like someone in a frenzy had been looking for a bra and found a hairbrush.

As she crashed about like a maniac, pointlessly searching, I wondered how she got dressed in the morning and marveled at her ability to arrive at work in clothes like she had pulled them out of a wardrobe.

Then, in the middle of it all, was a notebook. It didn't say "diary," but still, I shouldn't have read it, even though it was *just* a notebook. But, as Helen headed for the bathroom, I picked it up and it fell open onto a page—*sort of*—and I, without thinking, read . . .

Henry told me to go to the doctor's and get something for my hormones. Even though I told him they were fine, he didn't believe me. He seems to think that the menopause has turned me in to a man-hating lesbian with no brain, and all I needed were a few drops of estrogen and everything—meaning me—would be back to normal again.

We were sitting in his aunt's café, and he was talking to me like I was a two-year-old.

I wanted to tell him why I had left, why I couldn't go on with a man who barked orders at me like a sheepdog and, like the said sheepdog, expected me to obey. But when his aunt plonked a coffee under my nose like I wasn't there, I said nothing—the words were stuck.

Then he began to talk of his depression and how the split had made it diffi-cult for him to work.

"He doesn't know whether he's coming or going," said the pig of an aunt. "Such a hard-working man."

For a moment, I felt a twinge of guilt. He had lost weight, looked grey and worn out, and hadn't touched his roll . . . and he loved his aunt's sausage-filled rolls.

"Can't we try and be friends?" I said.

"Friends?" he said.

"Yes, maybe get some counselling, work out what went wrong—you never know."

Henry grabbed his roll and bit into it with venom; sauce squirted out the side of his lip. He was like a small boy not getting what he wanted.

I felt sad for him.

"The last thing I need is counselling. Either you come back or we go to a lawyer and that, on your so-called wage, won't be cheap."

Henry began to talk of lawyers and money.

"There'll be bugger all for you," he said. "You'll end up in some bedsit with nothing."

That's when I realized I didn't have to listen anymore—or go into that frig-gin' café ever again.

I turned the page...

Henry booked an appointment with a lawyer. I wanted to wait, get used to waking up on my own and the freedom of not being shouted at. But Henry insisted if I was leaving, then there was no point hanging around.

We met outside the lawyer's office.

He grabbed my arm. "The house is only worth forty thousand, which is technically mine. If you agreed to a small sum, we could have everything settled quickly."

I said nothing; there were no words in my head.

I never thought I would get away from him, and here I was outside a lawyer's office.

It was all so quick.

I followed him up the poky stairs and sat, silent, as he talked of a quick settlement and how we had both agreed.

I could see the lawyer was uncomfortable, annoyed. He didn't like Henry, I could tell. In fact, he was just waiting for him to finish, and then when Henry did, the lawyer explained that we needed separate representation, and I—me, his wife—was "entitled to, well . . . half."

Henry went green, or almost green. His jaw jutted, his fist clenched, he seemed to shrink, and for a moment, I felt sorry for him.

"But it's my money," said Henry.

"In Scotland, she is entitled to half," said the lawyer.

Henry nearly choked on his coffee.

They talked of different lawyers. I never said a word; it was like my lips had been stitched up.

"I can act for one of you," said the solicitor, "and give you a few phone numbers for the other. Now, which of you would you like me to help?" He pushed a few business cards across the table.

Henry grabbed the cards. "You can have her," he said.

The solicitor smiled at me, and for the first time since I could remember, I felt safe.

I followed Henry down the stairs. "You're not getting half," he said. "In fact, I'll make sure you get nothing."

I watched him walk away. He was talking through his backside; I knew it, and I had an appointment with a lawyer who also seemed to think so.

I stared at Henry's back as he stomped down the road, and the funny thing was, I felt nothing, absolutely nothing. Perhaps just a little lighter.

I closed the notebook. I had never realized Henry could be so cruel.

"Well, there's no zinc in here," Helen yelled from the bathroom.

She appeared at the door, scanned the floor, and tipped open a garbage bag. "Maybe in here?"

I looked at her. "Don't worry about it."

Chapter Seventeen

ZINC CREAM

"Mother knows best" is a crock of shit.

"I'm sure it was in there," Helen muttered.

She sifted through the clothes and books, then, in desperation, grabbed another bag.

"Or here." She fiddled with the tight knot, and when it refused to budge, she ripped at the sides; towels spilled out, followed by a bra and a hammer.

She was definitely not a systematic packer.

I slid the book onto the top of a box. "Forget the zinc," I said, but she didn't hear. Instead, she upended three large boxes onto the floor with a "maybe in here" to herself. Pots and pans crashed to the floor, followed by a glass bowl, which smashed onto the ground—glass flew everywhere.

We stared, and then without a word, Helen bent to pick up the pieces, flopped to the floor, and cried.

I sat next to her.

"Who cares about the zinc? Mum wouldn't have believed me anyway." I feigned a laugh.

Helen scraped a sock from the floor and blew her nose into it.

"I'm sure it was in that box"—she pushed it with her foot—"or that one." She turned to me with dried tears on her face. "Buggered if I know now."

"Do you want me to help?" I said. "Put things away?"

Helen didn't answer. Instead, she picked up a photo of her old home.

She was standing outside. Henry had his arm around her like he was hanging on a kite about to fly, and she, with a forced smile, looked like the grip hurt.

"When I first left Henry," she said, "I felt like a rock drilled into pieces, like the hole left when a tree is uprooted. There was nothing; it was like he had engulfed me like a giant octopus and sucked everything out."

I patted her shoulder.

"Everything was grey until I left him."

I picked up a few pots.

"He was always tooting at schoolgirls, eyeing up talent, commenting on their arses. Like I was invisible."

I looked about for more pots.

"I mean, what's that say about him?" said Helen.

"But you're not married to him now, you left. You were so brave."

She smiled. "Sunshine and color, that's what it was like when I left."

I looked about the room. How long would it take to sort?

"Everyone felt sorry for him, of course."

"And you too," I said.

"Me? As if. You know what his aunt said? 'He's weak, not like you—you're strong.' What the fuck is that supposed to mean?"

"Yeah, but the aunt's a cow."

She blew her nose.

"You should be proud of yourself," I said.

She looked at the sock as snot dribbled from the sides. I handed her a scrunched-up tissue from my pocket. I watched as she pulled it apart.

"Proud? Look at me, I can't even find a spot in this tissue to blow" —she sniffed—"let alone a pot of zinc."

I opened my old pot cupboard. "Do you want me to put these pots here, and maybe your dishes?"

She blew her nose.

The tissue crumbled under the strain, and I handed her a toilet roll, followed by another longer comrade pat on her shoulder.

"The girls in the belly dancing class thought you were fantastic," I said.

"Amy doesn't," she muttered.

I began to pick up the glass.

Helen pulled a broom from behind the sofa. "I used to envy you—your marriage to Steven," she said, brushing up the glass.

"He's a good man," I said.

"Then I got to know your mum."

I tutted. "She's a pain."

Helen stopped. "Poor you."

I began to tell her about Mum's middle child theory and how they always deal in leftovers.

Helen, now opening drawers and filling them, nodded. "She told me too. I had no idea what *leftovers* meant, but I didn't ask." She slammed the cutlery drawer, now full, shut. "Your Mum's explanations take all day."

"Sibling rivalry." I laughed. "She says she's the only mother on 'God's great earth' who brought up two daughters with no sibling rivalry. Funny enough, it was the only thing my sister and I agreed on: Mum talking through her arse."

Helen chuckled as she began to search for more things to put in the drawers.

"Sometimes I wonder if she's going mad. I even asked her," I said.

Helen laughed. "What did she say—don't tell me, I can imagine." She stopped. "She hates Neff, you know. All I have to do is tell her that Neff is coming around and she's off."

It was my turn to laugh. "Steven says they are too alike, too much into attention."

"Like peas in a pod," said Helen.

It didn't take long to clear a few boxes and make some floor space. As I emptied boxes, Helen found drawers and spaces. Finally, as she swept the bathroom, she shrieked . . .

"If that's a mouse, I'll sue that so-called fumigator, he charged a fortune."

Helen raced from the bathroom, thrust a jar of zinc in front of me, and shouted, "I found it. This will make her eat her cucumbers."

Mum, having looked after Baby Bea while I helped Helen, was beaming when I walked in, and I felt a little guilty.

Mum had been ill when I was born; it was Dad and her mother who looked after me.

It was natural for her to be a little obsessed.

I looked at her and George cooing over Baby Bea. Who was I to begrudge her some time? And Baby Bea had a right to enjoy her grandparents.

I was about to say something nice and warm—maybe even give her a tentative shoulder pat, along with a "how could I manage without you?"—when she turned to me.

"Don't worry about the zinc, dear. George got something from the nurse; apparently it's thrush. The nurse was surprised you hadn't noticed, but when I explained how you just moved and were a little fragile, she understood."

This time it was my turn to swear.

Chapter Eighteen

SEX AND TREES

Six months later . . .

When I first learnt to belly dance, I hadn't been touched by a man for ages, and even then, it was hardly memorable. I was gagging for it, and belly dancing filled the need—until I met Steven. Being with him was as delicious as chocolate and as easy as emptying a box of them.

He loved to touch and was so good at it.

His hellos were gentle pats and soft kisses. He'd stretch for my hand without thinking and cuddled in at night with each hand on my breast, and I always loved it—until Baby Bea came along. Now the last thing I felt like was sex, let alone being touched; when Steven slid beside me, I pulled away.

He never said anything; in fact, I thought he'd given up. Instead, he would glance at me with *how bad are things?* looks, and as for bed, I was always asleep by the time he came in, but we never talked of it. Instead, we skirted around the "no touching" issue with jokes about Mum's annoying comments and her sudden love for storytelling.

It was the last thing you'd expect from Mum.

Mum had never shown the slightest interest in performing. She rarely came to watch me dance, and when she did, she usually looked bored. Mum was more a sportswoman; now she was obsessed with telling stories. She even started to dress like a storyteller, and she assumed I cared.

Every Monday, she'd roll up dressed like a gypsy or a witch and scare the children with stories of "Legs" the pumpkin, and every Monday, George or I would take her.

"What do you think?" She'd pose in her latest outfit and, without waiting for an answer, wheel herself to the side of the car.

Then she started reading in the old folks' home, waking them from slumbering in front of the TV with a loud beat of her newly acquired drum. She spoke of head-chopping and blood-curdling fights, ballsy ghosts, and goblins that used "weapons of mass destruction like toothpicks," all in an animated way that had you forgetting she was in a wheelchair.

Some of the residents managed to stay awake just long enough to finish their biscuits. But that didn't stop her bragging; according to her, the staff just "loved her stories—way better than belly dancing."

When Neff heard, she was fizzing. She, like Mum, always had to be the best. Neff began to talk of the good ol' days when we performed for wrestlers, a feeling as lost on me as the ability to find anything in my new kitchen apart from empty co-op bags.

Neff worked in the takeaway and, rumor had it, tried to cook with a little spice herself; she even offered to come and cook for me. Apparently, Tenzam, the chef, had been showing her a few spice tricks . . . how to get the best from lentils with garam masala being the latest.

Steven said, "Any cook worth their salt knows about garam masala, and bragging about it is as pointless as bragging about using salt."

The lack of touching was making him, well, touchy.

"The last thing I want to come home to is both your Mum and Neff telling me how to cook," he said, "and the last time you touched spices, Baby Bea filled her nappies with something on par with nuclear waste."

I didn't say anything. He'd changed the nappy, but the thought of Mum coming around bragging about her latest story seemed worse than Neff and her spice tin, and I didn't argue when Neff offered.

Helen was outside chopping a tree down when Neff arrived. After six months of staring into the dark shadows of the forest and endless mugs of tea and coffee, we finally had a plan—a plan Helen was happy to take her anger out on.

Helen had been to a couple of anger management classes and seemed to think tree chopping was better than abusing parking attendants. And with the wedding in a few months' time and Amy giving her mother a wide birth, Helen was struggling with her emotions, keeping herself busy in swear mode—until Amy finally got her wedding dress . . . . . . with her father . . . . . . and it was Henry that told Helen.

Within hours of finding out, Helen texted me, "Those trees are coming down tomorrow . . . fucking bastard."

It didn't take a genius to work out who she was talking about.

Helen appeared the next morning. I was filling the kettle in my usual comatose early-morning way when I pushed open the curtains and there she was, clutching a chainsaw, inches from the window.

She tapped it . . . like I couldn't see her. "You got any fucking oil for this thing?" she shouted . . . like I couldn't hear her.

When Mum arrived, Helen was oiling the chainsaw and Neff was standing beside her talking of spices and hormones. Mum, unconvinced that I could successfully look after Baby Bea while watching Neff grind a touch of cumin, appeared with a basket of veg including her usual pumpkin, which according to her had great healing properties for my uterus.

The last thing I cared about was my uterus. Pleasure down there seemed as probable as Mum jumping from her wheelchair and chopping Helen's fallen trees into kindling while tap dancing.

Mum wheeled herself into the kitchen, followed by George. The first thing she spied was Neff's box of spices.

"Cumin is the last thing you need," she said. "What you need is soy. All the Japanese use it and look at them—who knows what age they are? *And* they don't even know what TENA Ladys are, let alone sell them."

I was about to query Mum's so-called "knowledge" of the Japanese and how many she had actually met when she glanced out of the window to see Neff, now prancing about the garden balancing a branch on her head like an elegant lumberjack doing a sword dance (if there were such a thing).

And Helen was almost laughing!

Mum threw me a look. "What the hell is she doing with a chainsaw?" She was about to say more when Neff appeared at the back door, posing with her stick, and Helen behind . . .

"Hi, Neff," said George with a wry smile.

"Hi, George," said Neff with a wry smile back. Working in the Taj Mahal often had that effect on Neff. The Taj Mahal, or Taj, was an Indian takeaway run by Tenzam, a small round man who many claimed was the real reason for Neff's wry smile.

"Coffee?" said Mum with a robust flick of the kettle, and without waiting for an answer, she began to spoon coffee into mugs.

She looked at Neff. "Sugar?"

"Me? Sugar? That poison never touches my lips," said Neff with a swing of her branch.

"A mere 'no' would have sufficed," muttered Mum, stirring with vigor.

Neff opened her spice tin and, with an exaggerated inhale, began a lecture on the ways of Asian women who, according to her, "hardly wrinkled, let alone dried up *down there*" and how "we could all do with a little turmeric." She laughed.

"Pfff," said Mum.

The whole genitals thing was beginning to make me feel sick. *Drying up—who cares?* I wanted to shout. *I don't even want to be touched.*

Instead, I began to search for biscuits to offer, and after watching me uselessly opening several cupboards, Helen found a packet.

The two of us stared out on the garden naked of trees. *The night will be shadowless,* I thought, as Helen looked at me with a "that feel better?" around my shoulder.

Steven walked into the garden, stopped at a tree stump, and stared.

Steven's not a garden man, and he seemed happy for the trees to be taken down on account of me moaning so much. When I say happy, I mean he didn't say anything when I told him . . . or rather texted.

I watched as he marched from one stump to another like the last thing he expected was to find no trees.

I was confused.

"He looks a bit pissed," muttered Helen.

"I don't understand," I muttered.

Then he caught Helen with her arm still around my shoulder, and he took on a darker expression which Mum called "seething."

I watched as he headed to the bedroom.

"What's up with him?" said Mum.

I shrugged. Waiting for him to cool down was my only option. Steven doesn't do angry, he does silent brooding, which, if handled incorrectly, will lead to . . . well, more brooding, followed by under-the-breath swearing.

"Hadn't you better go and see?" said Mum.

George muttered a "leave her be, she knows best."

Mum brushed him off with another "pfff."

"You won't get another like him, you know," said Mum, beginning her useless bench wiping.

"Leave her be," said Neff.

Mum, ignoring Neff, began to mutter *yet again* about "getting back into the saddle."

"Saddle?" said Neff to Helen.

Helen threw Neff a "typical" look as they headed back outside clutching hot coffee and biscuits, while I made my way to the bedroom; once Mum started on about saddles, she didn't stop.

Chapter Nineteen

THE ARGUMENT

Tree chopping kills more than just a tree.

When I walked in on Steven scrunching his jumper into a ball, I immediately regretted it. The last thing I was up for was an argument.

"I liked those trees," he said without looking at me.

"Oh? You never said."

"Said?" He eyed me. "Every time I say something to you, you cry."

I wiped a tear. Normally he'd hand me a tissue; this time he huffed.

"There's a tissue under the pillow." He gestured, then before I had a chance to lift the pillow, he thrust one at me with a "here."

I muttered a "thanks."

He muttered a "no worries," left the room, then paced back in.

"What's she got that I haven't?"

"What?" I sniffed.

"Her—my sister."

I was confused. One minute he's talking of trees, and now Helen . . .

"I mean, have I got rabies or something?" he said.

"No. I don't think I have ever mentioned rabies, have I?"

He pulled his jumper from the corner and, with an angry flick, shook it out of its ball.

"Have you gone all lesbian then?"

"Lesbian?" I said. "What are you on about?"

He tutted, folded his flattened jumper, tossed it onto the bed, and, with a "forget it," stomped into the bathroom.

I heard him crashing about, a flush of the toilet . . . then a shout: "I mean, if you are—just friggin' say so."

Steven was angry, I could tell by the flush of the toilet, so I stupidly rabbited on, which only made things worse. The more I talked, the more he huffed, and yet I couldn't stop. All my instincts were telling me to leave him alone, let him cool down, and yet I couldn't help myself. I had to talk . . .

"I feel nothing," I said at the bathroom door, "but I want to feel something."

He didn't answer.

"I've shut down, like a power plant with no . . . power."

Nothing.

I pushed open the door. Steven was scrubbing the toilet with a brush like he was scraping seven layers of paint off a tin roof.

"You have no idea," I announced.

Scrub, scrub . . .

"I feel so anxious."

"You said you feel nothing," he said, still scrubbing.

"It's like I'm in a Stephen King movie," I said.

He stopped. "What's Stephen King got to do with it?"

"Well . . . it . . . this house . . . it's so big and noisy. When I'm alone, it's just like a Stephen King movie: I keep expecting *It* to appear from behind a tree riding a tricycle."

"Don't be ridiculous."

"What?"

"There's no trees now, are there? You chopped them all down—may as well have chopped my penis off."

"There are still a few bushes," I muttered.

Steven shoved the brush into the holder, squirted way too much bleach into the toilet, and began scrubbing again.

"*It* didn't ride a bike. It was in that other movie about a couple in a house alone, and . . ."

He stopped, brush dripping. "Why don't you read Terry Pratchett then? That will take your mind off things."

"Too complicated. I can't even read a recipe, let alone a plot as complicated as this house's plumbing."

"What about a *Woman's Weekly* then?"

"I hate *Woman's Weekly*."

He tossed the brush into its holder. "I hate Stephen King!"

"You like Stephen King," I said.

"And you used to like me," he said.

"I still do," I said.

"I find that hard to believe. Every time I touch you, you recoil."

"It's nothing personal . . ."

"Like an electric shock."

"You're totally exaggerating. I don't move that fast."

"I don't see you recoiling from her," said Steven.

"You're overreacting," I said.

"I feel like a leper," he said, wrenching towels from the holder. He tossed them onto the floor of the bedroom and looked at me with a slumped sigh. "I just miss holding you."

I sighed. *Why the hell did I start this?*

"And there you are letting my sister . . ."

I started to cry. "It was a friggin' hug."

Steven huffed.

I blew my nose.

"Get back on the horse," shouted Mum as George told her to shut up.

"Does the whole world know about our nonexistent sex life?" said Steven. He pushed past me into the bedroom.

"My fanny's a no-go area," I blubbered. "I can't help it."

I blew my nose again.

"It's shut down, like a power plant during a power cut—"

Steven turned to me. "What?"

"—but when the lights come on, you'll be the first to know."

Steven, lifting his jumper and with a flounce, headed for the door. "Well, I just may not be here," he said.

Which I knew was a totally empty promise.

Mum and George heard everything, as did Helen and Neff, who left with a quiet "cheers" and a gentle door shutting.

I followed Steven into the garden, and as he began to pile up the logs with his jumper now slung around his shoulders like some sort of gay croquette player, I watched, not even offering to help.

I was too busy sniffing, and I could hear Mum and George in the kitchen.

"Poor guy, bet he hasn't had it for ages," muttered George. "I remember those baby days, never wanked so much since I was a teenager."

"Honestly," said Mum.

"What?" said George.

"Just because we share a bed doesn't mean you have to talk like a porn whatever."

"Well, it's true. I had the wrist muscles of a shot-putter."

"Now you're talking bollocks," said Mum.

Silence . . .

"I told her, didn't I?" said Mum.

"Hmmm."

"You'll never find another like him, I said."

"So you did," said George. "Big help."

"Men find it hard to, you know, understand the whole baby thing," said Mum. "Even someone like Steven."

George stopped. "Steven?"

"Well, he's almost gay, isn't he? Very feminine."

Gay? Steven? He's anything but, I thought and was about to shout as much through the kitchen window and then Steven caught my eye. Perhaps he'd taken it the wrong way.

Mum continued . . .

"I mean, there is touchy and well-over-the-top camp touchy"— Mum circled the kitchen—"but hating Stephen King? Who hates Stephen King?"

"He's just found out about the library," said George.

Mum stopped mid circling the kitchen.

"Library?"

"Yes. They are talking of closing it."

"Closing it?" said Mum. "But isn't Helen working on the roof next week?"

"Helen is working in the community centre next door, on the walls of gratitude."

"That bloody thing."

"Yes," said George, "that bloody thing."

"So she's not fixing the library then?"

"No."

"Bollocks," said Mum. "What about my storytelling?"

I looked at Steven, piling logs in a temper. *What about Steven?*

Chapter Twenty

THE DISHWASHER

It is not always the mother who has the "mummy genes."

Steven was quiet for the next few days, saying little but retreating into his study to work on his new book with a new character. Apparently, the old one had outlived its purpose.

When we first moved to our home, Steven's writing routine was as it always was: him in the kitchen occasionally reading out, waiting for my input. I knew all his characters and could help with the plots and back stories. Not now. I had no idea what he was working on. He never read to me; apparently, I had as much interest in his characters as I did in sex.

To be honest, my attention span was as short as a TV ad and just as compelling. The only thing that held my attention was my bed, and the only thing I felt comfortable doing was feeding Baby Bea. Once the pain stopped, I found breastfeeding as natural as blinking. I didn't have to do anything, just let her drink and zone out. I even had my favorite chair with a perfect view of the loch. Baby Bea tucking in was the best part of the day and hell mend anyone who interrupted, including Steven. It was my snooze-and-coffee time, my chocolate-and-staring-without-guilt time . . . and it usually soothed Baby Bea.

Except for last night . . .

Baby Bea woke several times and cried for what seemed like a decade, and this morning she was no better. She was whiny and hot and refused to be soothed. I jostled her about with a "come on, keep quiet" while uselessly piling dishes from one side of the sink to the other.

The place was a mess; I hadn't cleared anything since the bonfire. Six months on and I still struggled with the whole housewife thing, it overwhelmed me. Most days I spent on my own staring at the tree stumps in between feeds. Mum, now telling stories and trying to sort out the mysteries of Helen, was preoccupied. I hardly saw her, and when I did, she was about as helpful as a dishwasher in a power cut.

And as for Steven, he seemed to have lost patience; he was still in a mood and spent the last two days taking it out on his jumper until I shoved it in the machine. At which point he took to walking past the mess, tutting about the empty dishwasher and how any idiot could fill it.

He even made a coffee without making me one.

I threw together a sandwich for Steven and, forgetting that Baby Bea had just dozed off, shouted unnecessarily loudly. She jolted in my arms and began to cry, yet again.

"It's just a cold," shouted Steven, but I was beginning to panic. I had no idea what to do; it was Steven who seemed to have the "mummy genes."

I began shushing her as he walked in with an "I'm trying to write" look.

When he saw Baby Bea's red face, he took her from me.

"Does she need a doctor?" I said.

He slid her over his shoulder with a couple of gentle taps.

"Is it that rash again?" I said.

He looked at me with a *don't be stupid* look.

"I am only trying to help," I said. "I just don't know what to do."

"Have you fed her?" he asked.

"Well, yes, but she's not interested."

He looked into her face. "Have you tried some water?"

"She had a bit . . ."

Baby Bea let out a loud belch followed by another . . . then snuggled into the nape of Steven's neck.

He wiped her nose. "There, there, Baby Bea."

"She's never cried like that before," I said.

"Yes, she has," he said. He looked at her again, touching her forehead. "Has she had any medicine?"

"Shit, I forgot about that."

He pulled up a seat at the table, expertly slid a teaspoon of Calpol between her lips, and rocked her with another "there, there."

She began to doze, and he carried her to her room. I followed, watching as he slid her into her cot. Neither of us said anything, and we stiffly retreated back to the kitchen without a word. Steven, with a sigh, opened the dishwasher and began to fill it.

"I'll do that," I said.

He looked at me. I was still in my pyjamas. "Maybe you should get dressed first."

I didn't move. He'd be gone by the time I came back, the study door shut and him avoiding me. I wanted to make up, for us to be friends again . . .

"Sorry to hear about the library," I muttered.

He shrugged and pulled a pan from the pile of dishes and began to scrape imaginary burnt bits. "It should be closed in a month."

"Not if Mum has her way, she's started a petition."

Steven stopped mid pan scraping. "A few signatures are hardly going to make a difference."

"A few? She's got mountains of names—so Helen says."

Steven shoved the pan into the dishwasher and slammed it shut. The dishwasher chugged into action.

He looked about the kitchen. I could see him thinking, *Where to start . . .*

Let me try, I wanted to say. *Can we do it together . . . start again . . . help me, I'm lost!!!*

Instead, I made some stupid joke about finding clean clothes, which he greeted with a grunt.

I gave up and was just on the verge of heading to the bedroom when the dishwasher made a loud crashing noise.

I stopped. We both stared as water began to dribble from below, then oozed from the sides.

"Jesus," said Steven, uselessly grabbing a tea towel.

I looked under the sink, posed to turn the water off, as water burst the dishwasher door open. I skidded as water hit my legs and flooded the floor.

"Fucking hell," said Steven.

"Shut that door," I said, gesturing to the door leading to the passage as water trickled towards it. I swiftly turned the water off.

"Jesus," muttered Steven, staring at my drenched PJs.

Without thinking, I pulled out the dishwasher and began to investigate. Instantly at home with pipes and plumbing, I pushed and prodded as Steven, dragging the mop from the cupboard, stopped just shy of my behind.

As I grunted, manipulated, and prodded, he watched, handing me the odd tool that more often than not was wrong. Soon he was talking of the past . . . when we first met.

"Remember Oban?" he said.

I didn't answer.

"No one could sort that toilet."

I grunted, tussled free a connection, and threw a useless bit across the floor.

Steven picked it up and placed it in a bin bag.

"Except you."

I ran my fingers across a connection. *Where is the leak?*

"Your hair was long."

"Mum keeps on at me to cut it," I said, tossing the other piece of the connection.

Steven lifted it into the bag. "It hung down your back like silk."

I pulled a few tools from my box in the corner.

"You were like a mermaid."

"Can you pass me that . . ." I pointed to a wrench.

"You sorted the unsortable," he said, passing me a screwdriver.

I sat back and wiped my forehead. "We just need a few bits," I said. "Helen could bring them over."

Steven touched me on the shoulder. I turned to him.

He looked into my eyes with the sort of softness I hadn't seen for a while.

"Why don't you go back to work?" he said.

"What?"

"Why don't you help with the roof? It might make you feel better and Helen likes working with you."

"But Baby Bea . . . her feeds."

"Leave her with me," he said. "She's eating bits and pieces." He laughed. "They'll love her in the library. And your mum would be ecstatic."

I looked at him. *It was not that long ago when Steven said that my Mum was so unbearable he wanted to move to another country.*

"She could tell stories with Baby Bea," said Steven, "while you climb about the scaffold. I can call you when she needs a feed."

He touched my hand . . .

Come to think of it—it was me who mentioned moving to another country.

That night, as Steven talked of his new character, I listened and for the first time allowed him to wrap his arms around me, until Baby Bea woke. Steven brought her into bed and watched as I fed her.

"You were always my muse," he said.

"Oh?"

"So hard to write without you listening."

I stared at Baby Bea's chubby cheeks and ran a finger across them.

"You don't need me." I blushed.

"You! You are every heroine. Without you, I would still be writing shopping lists."

I kissed my daughter; her little blue eyes flicked open and she smiled. For the first time, I felt warm inside.

"Everyone has a dip," I said. "Perhaps you could write about that?"

Chapter Twenty-One

THE LIBRARY

Scaring children requires the absence of mobiles.

Steven was in the library the next day when Mum burst through the doors driving her wheelchair like a Roman chariot.

The library was empty apart from a robust-looking elderly gent browsing the free newspapers, a small woman hidden behind the mysteries shelf, and a young mother trying to control her toddler hell-bent on touching everything in sight.

"It's not Monday," said Steven without looking up.

Mum, ignoring Steven, circled the room like she was on parade, despite the lack of audience.

"This place will close over my dead body," she shouted.

"That could be arranged," laughed the elderly man.

"It's under attack," Mum said.

"Pfff," muttered a small voice from behind a James Patterson.

"And it is up to us to stop it," shouted Mum.

"Stop the council," snorted the elderly man, "that'll be right."

A toddler ran past making driving noises. "Come back," yelled his mother with a yank, swiftly wiping his wet mouth.

Mum stopped and, with a grim look, pulled a petition from her bag.

"I have proposed a sit-in," she said, waving the petition like a flag.

There was a flush of a toilet as the toddler's older brother burst out struggling with his zip.

The elderly man, pulling a face, made a nuclear waste joke as the young mother attempted to help one child while holding the other.

"Who's going to join me?" said Mum.

"I'm just waiting for the bus," said the small woman, peering from a Jack Reacher.

"Me too," said the elderly newspaper man as the toddler wriggled free and kicked Mum's tyre.

Baby Bea sneezed, pulled a face, then went back to snoozing as I placed her beside Steven. My first day back at work. I was excited.

Mum didn't notice; she was busy trying to scare the two boys with a story. A story that went way over the toddler's head, but not his brother's . . .

"Pumpkins imprison little boys, just for a laugh, but they bite their finger off one by one first."

The older brother made for another kick like he was going for a goal, and the petition, now hanging limply from Mum's hand, was in the way. He missed and fell, grabbing the petition as he tumbled.

"That's enough," said the young mother, dragging the two off with a flushed face.

Steven and I watched with an *our daughter will never behave like that* look as the mother pulled at the petition.

The boy was not for letting go; as she prised one finger, another clamped harder. Finally, petition ripped in half, she freed one section of it, followed by the other. Mum, with a snatch, muttered a curt "thank you."

Steven motioned to Baby Bea sleeping by his side. "You'd better go," he said.

I looked at Mum.

Steven's eyes followed mine. "I can handle this," he muttered.

❄

Helen, unaware of the political rumpus in the library, was emptying the van in the car park. I could see her through the window. We were fixing the roof of the community centre, which was next door to the library. Her job was to mend, from the outside, a leak in the roof, while mine was to make the mending invisible inside.

The hole was made by the accidental tumbling of the wall of gratitude by McFlaherty the Brave after a few too many.

McFlaherty was an artist who taught life drawing and was known as the brave for three reasons: his ability to take off his clothes at a moment's notice, his ability to argue with the community centre's board to allow nude drawing, and his habit of grabbing anyone who stood still long enough to model for his classes, including members of the board.

The wall of gratitude stood in the middle of the community centre, a square foyer which led to all the other rooms: a wall designed to celebrate "the good, the bad, and the ugly" (as Neff put it) in the community.

It had, in its time, exhibited photos and posters of the great yoga teachings of "Ida from the North" and "Sally from Lochgilphead"; vegan cookery classes (also from Sally); salsa classes (from Imogen, Neff's nemesis and probably the main reason for Neff's "the good, the bad, and the ugly" comment); the best of the Women's Rural Institute cake and clothes hanger decorations contests; the Scout, Guide, and Beaver Christmas parties; and more, including the odd small photo of Nefertiti and her belly dancing troupe (another reason for the "good, bad, and ugly" comment) . . . until plans for the renovation of the community hall were made.

The plans were proposed, agreed on, changed, agreed on again, and finally, pending budget cuts, postponed, and the wall of gratitude remained.

No one listened to Lumpy the janitor, who pointed out that the wall was only a pop-up wall, attached to the ceiling like a set of chimes, even when McFlaherty planned the yearly art show.

Every wall in the community centre was covered with still lifes, portraits, landscapes, and seascapes, along with the odd nude from the life drawing class, tastefully picked so as not to give away the model's appendage size or identity (which was mostly McFlaherty).

Every wall—including the wall of gratitude, a wall designed, as Lumpy put it, for paper-thin photographs, posters, and the odd business card.

Lumpy watched as the art group hung and rehung large framed pictures the weight of an elephant on the wall of gratitude.

"How about a nice light print?" he said. "Or a few posters . . ."

Nobody listened.

Finally, when McFlaherty hung a life-sized nude—oil on canvas, in a frame befitting a royal portrait—Lumpy "threw a wobbly."

"Don't be friggin' stupid," he shouted, pointing to the flimsy connections. When no one listened, he made a final "health and fucking safety" sermon, and when that didn't work, he made plans to be unavailable for the week of the exhibition.

McFlaherty, having spent the whole weekend hanging and rehanging pictures to please all in the class, tucked into the free wine at the launch with a "this looks fantastic" sigh. Until, that is, a committee member pointed out that the life size was as tilted as a drunk trying to adjust his kilt. Then McFlaherty, living up to his "the Brave," pulled up a ladder to adjust it and took not only the wall and its paintings but half the ceiling and part of the roof attached as well.

"I was only trying to save the show," he muttered, his head peering through the purple arse of a nude.

It took several days of clearing and a decent downpour of rain to discover where the leak was . . .

Chapter Twenty-Two

THE PLAN

Who listens to someone in overalls unless they're sorting your plumbing?

Mum sat in the library speaking to an audience of Steven and Baby Bea while the others escaped, and soon a plan was formed. A plan that she insisted Helen and I listen to as she circled her kitchen later that day.

We had just dropped her home from the library and she, mid circling, saw us heading for the door and blocked our only escape. She was riled; losing her storytelling gig meant more to her than anything, and she wanted us to not only listen but help.

Mum, using the sort of language that would silence a bar, fiercely barred the door as she ranted about those "council bozos" who were "as efficient as a comatose twat."

"They have no idea about money and budgets," she said. "Their idea of saving is to cut services so they can swan about their shagpile carpet—barefoot."

"Well, that's not strictly true," muttered Helen. "I think they have vinyl as well."

Mum, ignoring Helen, carried on. "They're never happy unless they're chopping something to pieces. *Well*," she shouted, "I'm going to chop their dicks to pieces!"

"Not all of them have dicks," I said.

She looked at me. "You're not taking this seriously, are you?"

Helen chuckled.

Mum was just about to expand on dick chopping when George arrived with an "I'm here" cough.

He stood the other side of the door waiting for Mum to move so he could enter.

Mum refused to be diverted.

"Your carriage awaits," he shouted.

Mum turned with a start. "Carriage?"

"The card game, Francis and her dips, remember?"

Mum pulled a face. "Cards at a time like this?"

"It's always this time," said George.

"But this is an emergency." She snapped, "I've hardly got time for Francis and her friggin' dips."

George, saying nothing, began to rummage for Mum's coat.

Every week they played cards with the Aces High Club, and every week Mum protested, until her first gin. The Aces High Club was where they met; Mum kept beating George, despite how many gins he poured her, and she still did . . .

George called it foreplay.

Tonight, they were to meet at the home of Francis, who according to Mum had the sort of nibbles that required a decent dinner beforehand.

George, clutching Mum's least favorite jacket, eased himself past Mum's chair barricade.

She huffed. "Francis and her dips—the last thing I need is a belly full of sardines and herrings." She stared at the coat. "Or that jacket."

"Fish is good for the brain." George laughed.

"Pfff," muttered Mum.

George let out an exaggerated "arrrrgh, fish, fish, and more fish," while Mum huffed.

"Oh, shut up, George—how can I possibly concentrate with a sardine stretched across an oatcake inches away?"

Helen and I laughed; we had heard it all before.

"Come on," he said. "Your audience awaits, and you can tell them your plans. Maybe they'll sign your petition."

"In that jacket? I don't think so."

"And I heard"—he pushed her to the door—"it's a full house."

Mum looked at him. "Full house?"

"Yes, everyone."

"Even Chubby?"

"Even Chubby," said George.

Mum's face lit up. Chubby, the local butcher, was the sort of gossip who spread stories on par with Facebook. If Mum had *her* on her side, then the whole of Argyll would know about the library by morning.

"You're a genius," she said.

And for the first time ever, George blushed.

The next day, inspired by a late-night viewing of Stephen King's *Pet Cemetery*, Mum dressed up like a ghostly pumpkin and decorated her wheelchair.

She, with the help of Helen and myself, attached a mile-high tombstone made from egg boxes, splashed "Mid Argyll—The Graveyard of Scotland" across it, then attached two skeletons made from coat hangers and bin bags.

For a week, she parked herself outside the library, the community centre, and the co-op petitioning, and when no one took any notice, she told stories.

Mum is hard to ignore when she tells stories, and as it was near Halloween, many thought she was part of it. Soon she had a following, a mixed bag of children, their parents, and library visitors. In fact, the library had become a ghost town, according to Steven.

George supported her.

He drove her everywhere, keeping her and her growing followers going with flasks of tea and egg sandwiches, coughing—loudly—when her language got too colorful.

"Sign my petition," shouted Mum, "join me on a sit-in!"

"What's a sit-in?" said one tot.

Mum burst into a round of "We Shall Not Be Moved."

❄

By the end of the week, Mum's protest arrived outside the Taj in an attempt to nab all the Friday-night takeaway customers. With an audience of ten, including two primary school sisters chanting "sign the petition" and Janice, their mother, trying to persuade them to "call it a day," Mum was causing a scene, which had most passing cars tooting.

Originally, Mum had arranged for her entourage to meet at Kilmory, a stately castle converted into a beehive of offices for the council headquarters.

Mum and her group planted themselves in the car park at the front of the castle. Their aim was to block all workers entering without first signing her petition.

She had forgotten it was a public holiday, and the only workers there were three self-employed builders working on the reception renovations . . .

After a curt chorus of "We Shall Not Be Moved," they headed for the Taj.

Helen and I were working on the community centre roof that Friday. We had almost finished when we heard about the takeaway.

Neff, who always worked on Fridays texted to complain that Mum was scaring off all the customers and the Chinese was doing a killing.

I didn't reply; there weren't enough swear words.

As Helen cleared up, I went down to move the "rabble," as Neff called it . . .

I arrived to find Mum singing "Ghost Town" by the Specials and George looking uncomfortable . . .

I noticed someone familiar: a policeman standing outside the police station just across the road . . .

Ten years ago, Mum had driven a car full of folk—including me—to Oban. I had a hangover from hell, and it was two policemen, Rathbone and Cocolder, who stopped us. Mum was still driving at the time and was, according to Cocolder, "breaking every rule possible and making a few new ones."

Mum, assuming they were barely out of school, treated them in a flimsy, offhanded way that nearly cut short our trip to Oban. Not that

Oban is anything to write home about, except we had tickets to see the American wrestlers, and thanks to my Mum, it nearly didn't happen.

From what I could remember, Rathbone was a decent bloke and it was Cocolder to be wary of. As I passed around George's egg sandwiches, I recognized that same steely glint.

The last thing I needed was for him to recognize me. From what I could remember, I had just finished throwing up . . .

Mum, however, wasn't wearing her glasses, and by the way she was carrying on, she had no idea. Before I could stop her, she was shouting to him, "Do you have any children?"

Cocolder stopped . . . he seemed to have no idea who was beneath Mum's pumpkin-painted face.

"'Cause if you do, you'll not get any storytelling, not if those *pricks* at Kilmory have their way."

George let out an overcompensating loud laugh as I tried with a few abortive "Mum!"s to shut her up.

I texted Steven.

"Quick as you can and bring Mum's glasses."

Chapter Twenty-Three

A BLAST FROM THE PAST

There is more to camouflage than face paint.

Steven took a long time to come due to Baby Bea's nappy, which, to quote him, was "an explosion of sticky stuff that required a packet of wet wipes, lubricant, and a decent soak in the bath to clean" (order unknown).

As I waited, the two sisters moved from skipping to pushing each other, and Cocolder moved from across the road to inches from Mum with a blank expression.

Perhaps we got away with it?

"Egg sandwiches?" I said, with my best innocent look.

"No thanks," he said. "I've some pakoras to pick up."

His squeaky voice brought it all back—the anxiety of Mum and her fuck-ups.

A car tooted just as Cocolder, hand on door, was about to enter the takeaway.

Mum gestured an "up yours" with her egg sandwich.

"Mum," I hissed, "will you stop with the finger gesturing?"

Cocolder stopped.

He turned to me, his dark eyes betraying nothing.

"You look better than the last time I saw you."

Chapter Twenty-Four

COCOLDER AGAIN

The good ol' days when we used to play "I can punch harder than you" . . .

By the time Steven had arrived, the two sisters had given up pushing and were now charging about like football players. Janice was at her "wits end," while most of Mum's entourage had disappeared, persuaded to leave with a free naan and Cocolder's grim stance.

Cocolder had not only remembered Mum but reminded her of why he had, to quote Mum, "put the kibosh on her driving" and Mum was riled to the point that even George could not control her.

"You should be shot," she snapped, ignoring the toot of the Glasgow bus.

"Shot, I hardly think so," said Cocolder coolly.

"What you did to me was a . . . discrimination, a discrimination against the disabled."

Cocolder began to describe her driving like a comedy sketch, which, until Mum threw him a look, had George laughing.

"How dare you insult my driving," she snapped.

"I am not insulting—"

"You try driving with legs like play dough," huffed Mum, "see how you do."

"—just stating the facts," said Cocolder.

"Facts? You make me sound like something out of the Carry

On movies. This is my audience"—she gestured to the sisters racing around her wheelchair—"and you just . . . just . . . humiliated me."

"I'm not dressed as a pumpkin," said Cocolder.

"Let's get you home," muttered George.

"I am saving our community," Mum said in a loud voice.

"From what? A roast dinner?" said Cocolder.

A passerby chuckled.

"She is dressed as Legs, the pumpkin," shouted the younger sister. "He eats little girls."

Her big sister pushed her with a "shut up."

"Time for tea," said Janice, attempting to drag her youngest.

"Time for you as well," said George, making to push Mum's chair.

Mum, ignoring George, began to call Cocolder a prick "like those in the council," while the sisters, ignoring their mother, began to push each other with a "shut up."

"Look," said Cocolder, "I just came for my pakoras. If you want me to arrest you, just say the word."

"You, arrest me, hardly. I am expressing my freedom of speech," said Mum.

"You are putting people off their takeaways," said Cocolder. "You should move."

"Yes, come on Beatrice," said George.

"Come on, Mum," I said.

"How about we get some chips?" muttered Janice. The girls were almost persuaded, about to leave . . . until Steven appeared, parking his car at the bus stop.

He and Helen charged from the car like there was a fire and they were the only ones with a hose, caught a glimpse of Cocolder, jumped back in the car, moved it around the corner, and appeared again, this time a little puffed.

"Hi, Steven," said the sisters in unison.

"We're saving the world," said the youngest.

Push, shove . . .

Steven, stopping just shy of the pavement, sighed, tripping over the two girls mid-scuffle.

Cocolder, now looking like he had been rubbed up the wrong way and was thinking of revenge, surveyed Steven.

"Where have you been?" I said.

"You try finding glasses in that bedroom," snapped Helen. "Not to mention the nappy from hell."

Steven, shaking his pale face, muttered, "Chemical waste."

"That's my wee one you're talking about," snapped Mum.

"Yes, and you're the one that fed her curry," said Steven.

"You fed her curry?" I said.

"It was only a korma, and she enjoyed it," huffed Mum.

"That stuff did not come from a korma," said Steven.

"Korma?" said Tenzam, appearing at the door. "There is something wrong with my korma?"

"Well, there is when you feed it to a baby," said Steven.

"You fed my korma to a baby?" said Tenzam.

"And the rest," said George with a glare at Mum. "I told you, but would you listen?"

Cocolder's face lit up. "I know you," he said to Steven. "Your driving would drive an instructor to drink . . . ha ha."

No one else laughed.

"Take up cleaning for a living . . . ha ha."

Still no one laughed.

I turned from Steven to Mum. "The rest? What do you mean, the rest?"

"Take a look in the bin." Helen glared at Mum. "That's where the true story lies."

"Is Legs in the bin, Mummy?" said the youngest sister.

Janice sighed. "Legs is just a friggin' story."

George grimaced. "Let's get you home."

Mum, with a *move me at your peril* glare, snapped. "I am not leaving till *he*"—she gestured to Cocolder with her now completely dried egg sandwich—"signs the petition."

Cocolder, with a bored look, pulled himself up into an *I'm in charge here* stance and turned to the group.

"Right, that's it. Shape up and ship out . . . there is nothing here."

"Come on," said Janice, attempting to drag her youngest.

"I want a curry," said the older sister.

"Nothing? Our libraries are dying, closed down like an out-of-date atomic plant, and you say there is nothing doing?" snapped Mum.

Janice stopped in her tracks. "Libraries?"

An elderly couple heading for the Indian stopped. The man, puffing, leaned on his Zimmer.

"You're in the wrong place—you should be up at Kilmory," he said.

"Kilmory? That place is empty, a new reception is being built," said Mum.

"Typical," said an elderly man.

"They've got some bruiser from Glasgow ripping up a perfectly good carpet."

"Typical," said the elderly man's partner.

Cocolder moved to open the door, then turned. "When I come out, I want youse"—he gestured to Mum—"gone."

"They're shutting the library?" said Janice.

"Yes."

"I thought it was the schools."

"No, it's the library."

"You said they were shutting the wee schools."

"I said the wee schools will be next," said Mum.

"You mean I have been waiting here all this time with this lot"—Janice gestured to her daughters shoving each other—"for a lousy library?" She grabbed one of the girls. "Stop that!"

Mum huffed. "The library is very important."

"You should have been clearer. I wasted my whole day supporting you . . . and . . . for what? A dump of a library no one uses?"

"Steady on," snapped the old man.

Janice glared at him. "Who goes to the library these days?"

"Well, I do," snapped the elderly man. "Where else can you wait for the bus in the rain?"

It was then that Henry appeared.

Chapter Twenty-Five

THE TAJ

Closing the library is discrimination against those who can't buy books.

Henry was a man hard to ignore. In his youth, he was an alpha man, fast, aggressive and silently seething; now, after years of drinking and grimacing, he was more a grumpy man with an invisible arse, an unshaven granite-like face, and black Rasputin eyes.

As he arrived for his Friday jalfrezi, he caught a glimpse of his ex and threw her a *you're the last thing I expected to see* look, followed by a smile that stopped at his lips.

Helen said nothing. The last thing she expected to see was her "garlic-hating, tight-arse" ex appear for a curry.

Cocolder greeted Henry like they went shooting together or something equally sinister, while Tenzam greeted him with a handshake, along with a "your table's ready," like they were at the head of a large queue.

Helen looked at me and mouthed, "Table?"

I shrugged as Mum, seriously riled, shouted, "There is no room for democracy in literature," stopping traffic, silencing the sisters, and causing Janice to let out a series of tuts, along with a "now what's she on about?"

"If you don't sign my petition, I'm going to have to chain myself to your belt," said Mum to Cocolder.

Cocolder, ignoring Mum, ushered Henry inside the takeaway.

"Did you see that?" snapped Mum to George.

George, who was now starting to grind his teeth, silently stared.

Henry gave a showy *you first* gesture to Tenzam.

"The nerve of them," hissed Mum.

George, face flushed, hissed, "Let's just *go home*."

Tenzam, spying the elderly couple hovering about the door, motioned them to go first.

The couple filed in, followed by a "you first" and "no, you first" from both Henry and Tenzam, until Henry, after a gentle push from Cocolder, followed the couple.

Tenzam looked at Cocolder, noted his *get in* gesture, and headed in.

The door closed behind Cocolder.

"Not one friggin' signature," muttered Mum.

"No wonder," snapped Janice.

George raised his voice. "I said we should go home."

"Home?" said Mum. "Hardly. That man is going to sign my petition, come hell or high . . . something."

"Water," snapped George, "and why does *he* matter so?"

"*He* just does."

"You are being ridiculous," George said with fire.

"He's right, you are," said Janice.

"Me? Ridiculous? We have to stop 'em from shutting the library."

"And how is going inside the Taj going to do that?" said Janice.

"Well . . . it just will . . . I know it," said Mum, looking strangely vulnerable.

"If you go inside, I am going home," George huffed.

"Now who's being ridiculous?"

"Don't call me ridiculous," said George.

I looked at Mum's smudged face paint; she looked small and lost. I felt for her. I wanted to wheel her into the Indian and shout, "Just sign the fucking thing."

But I didn't. Instead, I touched her arm, causing her to huff with a glare.

"Come on, let's go," I said.

"*Et tu, Brute?*" She sniffed.

"Baby Bea needs you," said Steven in a soft voice.

Mum, turning the back of her chair to us, shouted at the wall, "I'm going nowhere."

George made to push Mum to the car. She grabbed his arm and was about to say something when George let go . . .

"If you're staying, I'm going," he said.

"Brutus . . ." she muttered.

"Don't give me none of your Shakespeare shit. I have pushed you around all week in that smashed-up pumpkin get-up."

"Hardly *all* week," said Mum, "and it's a ghost get-up."

"Taken you to your friggin' card night, let you win."

"You didn't let me win."

"Persuaded them all to sign your stupid petition, which we all know won't make a blind bit of difference."

Mum flashed her chair around to face George. "How dare you."

"I will dare all I like. You know why?"

Mum pulled a *go on, tell me—as if I care* face.

"Because you have no gratitude."

"Pfff," huffed Mum.

"No sense of . . . of . . . how I help."

"I didn't ask you."

"Mum, stop it," I said.

George shook his head and, with an "I've had enough," stomped to the car.

"George . . ." I shouted.

"Come on, George," said Steven, who was now jostling a hungry-looking Baby Bea.

"Leave him," huffed Mum.

George slid into the car and turned the ignition on. We watched as he pulled away, his jaw clenched, staring ahead . . . except for Mum. She turned her wheelchair towards the takeaway and headed for the Taj door.

No one saw her push in until she was stuck halfway.

"Can someone give me a push?" she shouted, just as Amy and her partner appeared from the corner with a couple of wine bottles clinking in a co-op bag.

Helen's face fell.

"Mum," said Amy, looking uncomfortable, "what are you doing here?"

"What are *you* doing here?" she said.

"We're having an Indian with Dad."

Helen looked like she could smash a window, and then when she heard that Henry had been *shouting* them to a "sit-in Indian" the last few Fridays—to discuss the wedding—she looked like she could smash a greenhouse.

"He thinks he's helping," said Amy.

"Helping? As fucking if," she said.

"Since he gave up the drink, that's all he wants to do. He even gives us a lift home after."

"You've got to admire the guy," added Gary, Amy's partner.

"Giving up the drink," said Janice, "is not easy."

"Admire fucking *him?*" hissed Helen.

Jesus, I thought, World War Three on all fronts . . .

"Can someone give me a push here?" said Mum.

The two sisters, with a few giggles, pushed Mum in . . .

The door closed behind, followed by a crash, and pretty soon after, the fire alarm . . .

The next morning, Mum was in the hospital and George was nowhere to be seen.

Chapter Twenty-Six

THE BREAKING OF A WHEELCHAIR

How can the community carry on with services cut like an umbilical cord?

Helen was the first to go in.

Steven, clutching Baby Bea, and I followed . . .

Mum had skidded, swirled, and toppled—crashing into a tandoori mixed grill—and there was chicken shashlik everywhere . . .

Crunching on a sea of poppadums, we entered . . .

Mum, small and frail with a suspicious-looking twisted leg, was staring at the ceiling beside her upended wheelchair, wheels spinning maniacally.

The elderly woman, refusing Tenzam's "let me," was perched precariously on a chair and flapping her paper napkin at the smoke alarm.

And Helen and Henry, in sync, were silently wrapping towels about Mum like they knew what they were doing.

The kitchen porter entered, wiping his hand on his apron, pulled a broom from the corner, and knocked the alarm from the ceiling, sending it flying across the room.

"Jesus," muttered Steven.

"Any more towels?" said Helen, without looking up.

"Here," whispered Henry.

She slid one under Mum's head, tenderly picking fried rice from her forehead. "Comfortable?" She smiled.

Mum moaned in pain.

Tenzam bent into her face. "The ambulance is coming."

Mum, dazed, looked up. "George?"

"He's gone, Mum," I said. "But I'm here."

"Bugger," she muttered.

Mum spent the night in the hospital. Her wheelchair, thanks to a tray of dips, several Cokes, and a pint of Indian beer, was out of action.

The ambulance had taken several hours to arrive, in which time Mum flitted in and out of painful consciousness, talking about the "war on Libraries," and "where would we be without books."

Then, when her head began to "bang like a drum," she went all hallucinatory, shouting "newspapers are being read by headless chickens" at which point Cocolder headed into the kitchen, shouting for an ambulance on his radio.

"It's five minutes from here—what are they doing, pumping up the tyres?" he shouted, then returned shamefaced, explaining that there was "a road accident requiring more than one ambulance."

Steven took Baby Bea home, while I waited for the ambulance and Amy explained what she saw . . .

The tombstone, having been pushed into a smaller shape by the sisters to fit through the doorway, had toppled about Mum like falling bricks as she burst in.

Mum couldn't see a thing.

She collided into the counter as the skeletons, flapping like scarecrows, sent a tray of drinks flying.

"Beer spewed everywhere," said Gary with dramatic animation. "Over your Mum and her wheelchair."

"Fizzing," as Amy put it, "the controls . . ."

The restaurant was a tiny place, with several tables placed as best as possible, making movement between tables limited to stomach-held-in side-walking.

A movement which Neff, Tenzam, and the regulars were expert at.

Mum, having never been in the restaurant, was no expert; she had no idea that a table was spitting distance from the door, and as she tried to control her chair, she, catching the tablecloth, set off a collision of movements that in the end was the demise of two deluxe mixed tandoori grills, a tray of dips, and a korma-splattered lap of the elderly gentleman.

"I guess those wheels aren't slip proof after all," muttered Amy.

"Nothing is," said Gary, "when spinning like a Catherine wheel, which apparently is the effect of beer and Diet Coke on the electrics of an old-fashioned motorized wheelchair."

Before Mum could stop the spinning, the drinks cooler was hit, toppling dips onto Tenzam's path, who, entering with two smoking plates of tandoori mixed grill held high above his head, skidded with the precision of a goat on ice—sending the tandoori and Mum flying.

As smoke filled the room, the wheelchair zoomed towards the kitchen. Mum, who, according to Gary, "looked like a startled chicken," grabbed the nearest thing; the tablecloth underneath the elderly gentleman. Before the gentleman could grab his Zimmer, korma, like melted play dough, had plopped onto his lap.

Mum crashed into the plate warmer and ricocheted into the toilet door, which then propelled the wheelchair backwards and Mum onto the floor between two steps.

And the older sister filmed it all on her mobile, until her mother clipped her over the ear with a "now look what you've done."

"Jesus," I muttered, peering into Mum's sweaty brow.

The next day, the sisters, clutching flowers, visited Mum. Mum was snoozing at the time, but Janice was adamant they were to do what they came to do.

"Go on," she said.

The sisters gingerly slid the flowers onto her bed and made to run, when Mum, with a snort, woke up.

"A daisy from a daisy." She smiled, high on painkillers.

"Say sorry," snapped Janice.

Mum held up a wobbly hand. "All in a day's work."

"Tell her you're sorry," said Janice.

"Sorry," muttered the sisters in unison.

Mum's eyes fluttered shut; she snored.

"She keeps doing that," I said.

Mum's eyes flashed open. "George," she shouted.

"He's not here," I said.

"George? Is that you?"

"Mum, it's me."

She grabbed my hand and nearly broke it. "We have libraries to save—put it away."

"Mum, it's me," I said.

"Go on, tell her," Janice said to her girls.

"I think she's gone back to sleep," I said, feeling for the sisters.

The elder sister shifted uncomfortably.

"I can't think with that thing dangling . . ." Mum laughed manically.

"She's hallucinating," said the patient in the next bed, "been doing it all night."

The patient who went by the name of Madge was a middle-aged woman with unruly straw-blonde hair and a white hospital nightdress that gaped at the back. She looked like the sort who drank vodka without any tonic and couldn't stop at one.

Madge rang the bell. "She's doing it again," she shouted.

Janice pushed her daughter forward. "Go on."

"Yes, go on," said the youngest.

Janice threw her a look. "And you can keep quiet."

The nurse appeared at the door with a huff. "It's the painkillers," she shouted from the doorway, "it'll wear off soon."

The nurse looked at me. "Then *she* can go home."

"Finally," snapped Madge with a dramatic collapse onto her back. "I am exhausted."

"I said put it away, George . . ." Mum laughed and began to snore again.

"It's all away," the nurse shouted at Mum, still by the doorway. She smiled at me, her face softening. "Wouldn't worry, happens all the time."

"Well, that's a big help," huffed Madge, now staring at the ceiling.

Janice nudged her daughter. "Tell her!"

The oldest sister stepped forward.

"I'm sorry, I shouldn't have done it . . . didn't mean to, won't do it again . . . I just . . ."

She looked at her mum; her mum nodded for her to go on. With a deep breath, she raced through her words . . .

"I put it on Facebook—but I was going to take it off again . . . meant to . . . but . . ." A tear rolled down her cheek. "Too late now."

Silence . . .

"George?" Mum peered at the ceiling.

Neff rustled in, dumped a box of after-dinner mints by Mum's bed with a "from Tenzam," pulled up a seat, and looked at me.

"Everyone's seen it," she said.

"What?" I said.

"Facebook! It's on Facebook."

The two sisters disappeared behind their mum's back. This time Janice shielded them.

"Your Mum on *that* wheelchair, Tenzam's skid, the fire alarm flying across the room . . ."

She sat back and looked at her audience; even the nurse was listening.

"I'm not in it, of course." She huffed. "I had a korma, two jalfrezis, and a madras to deliver; by the time I was back, it was all over, bar the mopping."

She stopped.

Janice was in full blush.

"But I must say," said Neff, "whoever filmed it did an excellent job. First-rate comedy."

"Right, girls, let's go," said Janice.

"Facebook?" murmured Mum.

"It's okay, Mum, go back to sleep," I said.

"There's a video on Facebook?" asked the nurse.

"George! George! George!" shouted Mum.

Madge let out a loud tut, then tossed a paper cup at Mum; it bounced off her shoulder.

Mum's eyes flashed open. "The codpiece. I dreamt it was on Facebook."

"Codpiece?" said Neff. "I thought we got rid of that thing."

Chapter Twenty-Seven

ANOTHER BONFIRE

When it comes to a codpiece, age is no barrier.

Neff's codpiece was a fine piece of equipment: the sort of equipment that inspired songs and poems, that spun legends and jokes and the sort of equipment Neff had tossed aside like an old bra.

It was ten years ago when I first saw it. Mum and I were at a wrestling match, and Neff was set to perform. Neff had fallen out with her then-partner Rodger, and he was determined to win her back by abseiling in the middle of a wrestling match wearing the codpiece over a panda suit . . .

Why Mum was hallucinating about that, I had no idea.

As I arrived at Mum's house pondering Neff's exaggerated codpiece stories (usually told after way too many home brews), I caught sight of Helen peering from the kitchen window.

She waved me up. She seemed anxious and wanted to know how Mum was, and when I told her about the codpiece, she feigned a laugh.

"Oh, *that?*" she muttered.

I told her about the wrestling match as she, deep in thought, prepared coffee. She wasn't really listening. She was in a thoughtful mood that only performing first aid with someone who abused you could do. It can be very confusing when someone who has treated you badly for years acts like a decent human being. It can shake your defenses harder than a car crash.

I watched her pull coffee from the cupboard. Beside it was a bottle of wine.

She stared at the wine . . .

"Henry was visiting your Mum when I walked in," she muttered. "He was holding her hand like they were bosom buddies."

"That'll be the painkillers," I said.

"He looked so . . . human," muttered Helen. "He even smiled at me."

"It's only natural after, you know . . ."

"Like he meant it," said Helen, "and I hate to say it, but I smiled back."

I was about to say "It's only natural" again and stopped. She looked confused and, it seemed, disappointed in herself. I had no idea how to help, so I poured us both a glass of wine, pulled a box of chocolates from Mum's secret stash, and began to talk about the first time I saw the codpiece.

I described with as much exaggeration as possible how Rodger, a man Helen knew as the mildly camp artist, abseiled into a hall full of children young enough to think an expanding codpiece was a jack-in-the-box in the wrong place.

She slurped her wine, staring into space.

"Abseiling to him was like peeling a banana. He was in a circus once, you know," I said.

"Hmmm," she muttered.

"I mean, I know it's hard to believe when you look at Rodger now, shacked up with Shifty."

She nodded.

"But back then he was as straight as you and me, and not only that but mad about Neff . . ."

Helen looked at me. "Doesn't he paint penises?"

"Well, yes, but there was a time when he painted other things . . . women's things."

Helen threw me an *as if* look.

"And that night he was determined to win Neff back—in a panda suit," I said.

Helen stopped. "Panda suit?"

"No one noticed at first. He was just a pimple in the distance . . . until the crowd saw him a few feet above the ring, and that's when he opened his legs—"

She gulped. "You're taking the piss."

"—with the Proclaimers on full volume."

She spluttered. "The Proclaimers? Get out of here."

I slid a Turkish delight into my mouth, letting the image form in Helen's mind. She took a nut cluster.

"The codpiece sprang forth like a jeweled jack-in-the-box—" I said.

Helen stopped her glass inches from her lips. "To the Proclaimers?"

"—bobbing with each pelvic thrust."

Helen almost laughed.

"Neff called it his *bugle*," I said.

"No way," said Helen.

She drained her glass, filled it along with mine, leant across the table, and whispered, "I found *it* when I was looking for your Mum's glasses."

She sat back.

"It's like something out of a *Carry On Henry VIII* film—if there ever was such a thing."

"Henry's codpiece is a mere toothpick compared to this thing in motion; it is the pinnacle of all phallic art," I said.

Helen slid another nut cluster into her mouth, then pushed the chocolates my way.

"I can't believe Mum and George have that thing, let alone use it," I said, curious and yet squeamish at the same time.

"It takes a few gins," she muttered.

I stopped. "What do you mean?"

"Walked in on them once."

"Don't tell me any more," I said.

"And he wasn't singing any Proclaimers song."

She chuckled, then stopped. We stared at each other . . .

Helen pulled a white truffle from the bottom of the box and opened it. I watched her slide the truffle between her lips.

"Follow me," she said, dragging me and several chocolates to Mum's bedroom . . .

I had never really seen the codpiece up so close, and there it was: a magnificent piece of contracting and expanding equipment, studded with green and red baubles and a red gem the size of a tennis ball at the tip.

Helen pulled it out.

The codpiece swayed like a jeweled palm tree; she flicked a switch and the tip pulsated like a disco light.

Helen put it on, twirled a few times, and finished with a robust pelvic thrust.

She laughed like a schoolgirl.

"When Neff and Rodger split," I said, "they argued over that . . ."

"No wonder," she laughed, jerking her pelvis at the mirror.

"Neither wanted it," I said.

Helen stopped. "Seriously?"

"In the end, Neff donated it to the charity shop."

"It's magnificent," Helen twirled.

The top layer of Mum's milk tray was now finished, and as I poked about the second layer, Helen sat on the bed, the erect codpiece upright between her legs.

"Henry waited for me outside the hospital. He was standing by his car."

The codpiece pulsated.

I sat beside her.

"It was like we were still married."

She shifted; the codpiece wavered back and forth.

"So confusing." She sighed.

I put my arm around her and hugged her.

"I think I should stop being so angry," she said. "It's not helping."

Later that afternoon, Steven drove into the drive.

Helen and I had finished the wine and were washing up. As I watched Steven ease Baby Bea out of the car, delicious memories of

Steven and I came flooding back . . . for the first time in ages I felt like my old self again, desperate for a Steven hug.

Helen stopped.

"Maybe you should borrow it. It might help, you—you know, with getting back on the horse?" She laughed. "I certainly feel like getting on one."

I waved to Steven; he, with Baby Bea's hand, waved back.

"Have you seen the video?" he shouted.

Chapter Twenty-Eight

VIRAL

The world's gone mad.

Amy's wedding was in two weeks, and Helen was a changed woman. It was like she had deposited her anger at the Taj, along with the towels they'd wrapped around Mum's bleeding leg, and it was all because of the video.

The Facebook video had gone viral and caused quite a stir. A stir that involved a great amount of attention towards Mum and Helen; attention which Mum didn't want and took Helen by surprise . . .

Helen and I arrived at the hospital to pick up Mum.

Mum, with an *I've been ready for a century* look, was sitting in her day clothes, polished and pissed off with a small plastic bag at her feet. Her bed was neatly made for the next arrival, and Madge was glaring at her like a dog at a rabbit hole. Madge was the last person you would want staring at you; her white-powdered face, painted-on eyebrows, and lipstick-stained teeth screamed *unhinged*.

Mum started with "Thank god you're here," while the cleaner nabbed Helen.

Mum, unable to move from her chair, had already seen the video; the cleaner had stuck her phone under Mum's nose with the volume on full.

Mum was still recovering, using the sort of language that would make a porn star blush, as the cleaner, along with Helen, watched the video in rapt awe.

By the third replay, Mum had had enough.

"Stop looking at that pile of puke," she snapped.

The cleaner looked up. "This woman here"—she gestured to Helen—"saved your bacon."

Mum huffed.

"A real hero," said the cleaner.

"Pfff," said Mum.

Helen blushed.

"You'd be one leg less if it wasn't for her," said the cleaner.

Helen shifted uncomfortably. "Wouldn't say that," she muttered.

Madge, still focused on Mum with a glare that would stop a wild dog, began to shout about her Sunday takeaway and how it was "completely fucked because of *her!*"

Mum threw her best *go shrivel up and die* look, and Madge threw her best one back, looking scarily like a mental Bette Davis.

"And as for that Henry" —the cleaner sighed—"amazing . . . he knew what he was doing."

"He was always good in an emergency," muttered Helen.

"I'll not see a jalfrezi for at least a century." Madge looked at Mum. "And as for a pakora"—she shook her head—"may as well blow smoke up my arse."

"The Taj is only closed for a week or two," Mum yelled across the room.

"Aye," Madge yelled back, "and the rest—" She stopped as a nursing assistant entered wheeling a dilapidated wheelchair.

"Your carriage awaits." The assistant smiled.

Mum eyed it with suspicion as it squeaked to a halt by her side.

"How can I get about in that?" she said. "I've a wedding to go to."

The assistant's face fell. "Well . . ." She sniffed. "It was good enough for Lady Campbell."

"Aye, good enough for Lady Whats-her-face," shouted Madge.

"Lady Campbell is as *with it* as you are," snapped Mum.

"Up your arse," shouted Madge.

"Up yours," shouted Mum even louder.

Madge gave Mum the finger and was just in the middle of an *up yours* gesture when the assistant blocked her with a curt swish of her bed curtains.

Mum silently huffed as she made to sit on the chair.

It was the sort of manual wheelchair that wheeled like a shopping trolley full of cement and, according to Mum, was just as comfortable. It was like pushing through quicksand; by the time I wheeled her to the car, I was puffed and red-faced and Mum was huffing with indignity.

Mum was silent as we headed home, grimly staring at the windscreen. As we pulled into the drive, she looked up at the window with a quiet "have you heard from George?"

Neither of us answered; George was nowhere to be seen.

"He'll be back," she said, "within the week."

Helen joined her ex at Amy's last pre-wedding "everything is going to plan" meeting.

The meeting was held in the Argyll, the hotel that Shifty owned and Rodger helped run. Rodger served them cordon bleu fish and chips, along with his special reserve, homemade tartar sauce, and the "house" Prosecco.

Helen, as she put it later, tried not to imagine Rodger in his codpiece, especially when he popped the cork . . .

"Rodger's codpiece is burnt in my mind," she said. "In fact, whenever I feel angry, I just close my eyes and chant 'codpiece'—how can you be angry saying that?"

We were standing on Mum's drive at the time, making jokes about "high-rise batter" and "Rodger's bugle," until Mum wrenched open the window and emptied a tea pot inches from us—

"I can hear every friggin' word," she shouted.

—and slammed the window shut.

I guess the last thing Mum wanted to hear was anything about the codpiece . . .

Mum was in a state of shock. She was on the front page of the local newspaper, in an article named "The Poppadum Tapes."

"The ability of chicken shashlik to spread is incomprehensible," wrote the reporter, along with many other witty remarks and three photos: one of Tenzam and the elderly gentleman, still in his korma-splattered trousers; one of the kitchen porter, pointing to the remains of the fire alarm with his broom; and one of Mum . . . looking like an electrified chicken.

Mum glumly stared at paper and sighed. "In front of that Cocolder, too . . ."

She looked at me.

"I wasn't always in this friggin' wheelchair, you know. There was a time when I was like you."

She eyed me . . . "Well, more your sister."

"You mean slim," I said.

"Nineteen-inch waist," she muttered, tossing the paper into the bin. She huffed. "You know, if George phoned me now, I'd tell him to shove off."

"I believe you, Mum."

"I would," said Mum.

"I said I believe you."

"I mean, what sort of friend is he in my hour of need?" said Mum.

"Indeed," I said.

"Everyone is laughing at me."

"Thought you didn't care what folk thought of you."

"Everyone cares, they are just talking bullshit if they say they don't."

She stopped.

"Except for Neff—she's a narcissist."

"I'll tell her that," I muttered.

"You do, cause I'm not going out, not in this friggin' cheap-as-chips wheelchair, and no amount of lipstick will persuade me otherwise."

Chapter Twenty-Nine

SILENCE

Silence is deadly in an argument.

Every day, Mum moped about the kitchen window looking out onto the drive. Refusing to go out, she sulked; Mum hadn't heard from George in a week, and it was not like him.

George's breaks from Mum were always accompanied by daily texting and phone calls. The two of them would banter for hours about who was right, until finally George would arrive like nothing had happened and take Mum to the Aces High Club cards night.

This time there was no texting, just silence; George's phone went straight to voice mail and Mum looked scared.

"Why don't you call?" I said, regretting the brutal sound of my voice.

"Who needs him?" she said, feigning an odd smile, and I tried to believe her, until the Aces High Club night.

Mum, posed with her jacket on the back of her chair, waited in the kitchen.

I wanted to say something: that perhaps George may not come, that maybe she should try and apologize instead of leaving messages about how much fun life was without him.

I didn't. Instead, I told her what Baby Bea was up to until I could see the effort of forcing a smile was waning on Mum.

"Hope you win," I said, leaving.

She didn't answer but grimly stared out of the window like he would pull up any minute.

The next day, the jacket was still on the table, along with a bottle of whisky and an empty glass. Mum was nowhere to be seen. Normally she'd be up making coffee, swearing. Today she was still in bed, lying in a small huff in the dark.

"You okay?" I said.

"Leave me alone."

"Can I get you anything?" I said.

"No," said Mum.

"Was it a good night last night? Did you win?"

Mum told me, "to shut up."

I went back to the kitchen. Helen was by the kettle.

"He didn't come," whispered Helen. "I saw the light on and went up; there she was, coat ready—"

"I see," I muttered.

"—and before I had a chance to say anything, she told me to shut my mouth, help her to bed, and 'don't tell anyone, not even Sheryl.'"

Mum didn't come out for days.

No one knew where George was, including his sister, Morag, who blamed Mum and her "verbal abuse."

"You should be ashamed of yourself, the way you treat him," she said. "He's a saint, and you just take advantage. Just because you're in a wheelchair doesn't mean you can treat folk like . . . well . . . the way you do."

Mum feebly defended herself. "It's just banter," she said.

"Banter? Banter? If what comes out of your mouth is banter, then what comes out of my tap is piss."

For the first time ever, Mum had no answer. Instead, she glumly listened to George's sister, a woman who rarely swore, then retired to her room.

It was like all the stuffing had left Mum. Even Baby Bea didn't cheer her up.

She wanted to be left alone, for everyone to "bugger off," and as for the wedding . . .

She told me to stuff it in several places, most of which were painful.

At first, the idea of Mum not going to the wedding seemed like bliss: a whole day without Mum and her annoying ways.

Mum was a pain in public; she had a way of introducing me like I was a disappointment. If I was quietly standing, she'd say, "What's up with you?" If I was on my own, she'd tell me to "Go talk to so and so," and if I dared to have a glass in my hand it was "Another drink? Are you sure?" And now with Baby Bea, it was even worse . . .

For once, I could spend a day without the constant questions about what she was eating.

Steven was ecstatic. "Thank God," he said, "you can wear that blue outfit with the cleavage and she'll not be coming up all night tucking napkins into it."

"I am not sure I'll fit into that," I said. "In fact, I am not sure I want to."

The blue outfit was a suit along the lines of my getting-married yellow trouser suit, which Mum called my "canary outfit." She hated them both, claiming that I was "showing too much." Of what, I had no idea—I mean, it's a trousers suit—but in Mum's eye, any hint of chest was the equivalent of going topless.

I, idly wondering if I could fit into the suit, let alone feed Baby Bea in it, muttered something about "wearing a tent."

"Why a tent?" said Steven. "Let's make it a marquee."

"Oh, ha ha," I said.

Steven said nothing.

"There's nowhere for my breasts to hide in that suit," I said. "They will be out there screaming "feed time.'"

Steven threw me a *hardly* look. "I take it you're wearing a bra."

"Well, yes."

"So, they'll be under control . . . more's the pity."

"What?" I said.

"I said you've got it all under control, and Baby Bea's eating . . . she loves her food."

"Mum hates that suit," I muttered.

"I love it," said Steven.

Steven and I began to look forward to our day together. Steven almost looked happy. Occasionally he would stretch to touch my hand, and sometimes I let him; I was starting to feel almost normal.

And then, a few days later, he found the codpiece.

Chapter Thirty

THE CODPIECE

A codpiece by any other name still gets a laugh.

teven walked into the kitchen and there it was, snuggled beneath the fruit and veg bag, and I had no idea . . .

After the "I want to be alone" episode, I continued to try and cheer Mum up and visited her every day.

When I finished work, I'd pull into Mum's drive, stare at the empty kitchen window, help Helen clear out the van, look back at the kitchen window, and usually, with a long sigh, head up.

The thought of going in sapped me.

She didn't want me there—she didn't want anyone, it seemed—and yet, for some reason, I felt compelled to go in.

I wanted to help her, give her all the advice and nagging she had given me when I had crumbled, given in to solitude and darkness. But when I saw her sad face, I couldn't. Her nagging never helped me; if anything, it stirred things up, made me feel worse.

"I want to be alone," she said, "just me and the BBC." Apparently their sports channel was way better than Sky.

I'd never seen her like this: sulking in the dark, glued to the TV. But then she'd never been rejected before, let alone videoed dressed as a ghost pumpkin.

I slid a get-well card near her arm. She didn't look at it—not a reaction, not even a "get stuffed."

"It's from your storytelling fans, do you not want to read it?" I said.

She stared ahead.

I put it beside the other cards from the old folks' home and the Aces High Club.

Nothing . . . not even a glance. It was like she didn't see me.

"Mum?" I whispered.

"And you can take that shopping with you," she snapped. "I don't need it."

She flicked the channel.

"Shopping?" I said.

"Yes, Helen seems to think I am fading away . . . God knows what *you* think."

"What do you mean by that?" I said.

She paused the TV and looked at me. "Sheryl, you're an idiot. Why did you let them video me?"

"What?"

She turned back to the TV. "Just go away."

I stared at her as she flicked the channel.

"What was I to do?"

"You should have stopped them," snapped Mum.

Silence.

Mum sniffed.

"Do you want me to bring Baby Bea?" I muttered.

"No."

"You want to be alone?"

"That's right," snapped Mum, "I do," and she turned up the TV.

"But you love Baby Bea," I shouted.

Nothing . . .

"Don't you?"

"Who gives a shit," muttered Mum.

"What?" I said.

She didn't answer.

I watched as she shifted her body so her back was facing me and, with a sigh, left.

I stopped in the dark hallway.

My fault? Always my friggin fault?

I wanted to go back and yell, "*Fuck you!*" I wanted to make her look at me so I could say it again, even louder and uglier . . . but I didn't. Something, like it always did, stopped me.

Confused and annoyed with myself, I walked into the kitchen with, for the first time, no tears.

Helen handed me the shopping. "Take it. Don't worry, I'll check on her," she said.

"She is so callous—horrible. Why? I mean, pushing me away, bawling me out for caring—"

"You don't deserve it," said Helen.

"—I mean, what have I done?"

"Nothing, it's just the way she is. She knows you'll come back."

"She called me an idiot," I said.

Helen looked at me with soft eyes. "Go and enjoy your baby. It's Friday night, have some fun for a change."

I lingered, saying nothing.

"It's not easy—not to give a shit," she said. "It takes all your energy. Every time Amy talks about Henry, I want to not give a shit—but I don't. I have to go away and . . . recuperate . . . kill a pillow."

I poked at the shopping.

"Your Mum just needs time," said Helen.

I fumbled with the bags.

"And maybe a stranger, someone she's not close to . . . someone she has to be . . . well . . . civil to."

I arrived home and looked out into the garden to see Baby Bea sitting in the winter sun watching Steven poke an impressive fire. He had been home all day, clearing the garden, decorating the tree stumps with pots of plants, shells, and rocks while Baby Bea watched on a blanket, her golden curls ruffling in the wind.

She giggled.

"You weren't long," Steven shouted.

I smiled; it was a delicious sight. They both looked so happy, the complete opposite of Mum and that damn house. I dumped Mum's shopping in the kitchen and went out to join them.

"How's Beatrice?" he said.

"The same." I sighed. "And she won't even consider a doctor."

"Give her time," he said. "You never know, George might turn up."

"If only," I said.

I looked at Baby Bea's sparkling eyes and picked her up. I was beginning to feel quite at home with Baby Bea. She loved to laugh, and making her was so easy. She had a special look just for me, and as she threw me one of her best, I began to talk of Helen and her hidden depths. Steven, with a *tell someone who doesn't know* look, talked of food and cooking.

My stomach began to rumble; the thought of Steven's cooking made me hungry.

"Stay here with her," he said. "I'll make something that we can eat out here."

I didn't argue. Steven's cooking is beyond description; he can make baked beans taste fantastic. He can open a can of chickpeas, pull out a limp leek, add a few herbs, and before you know it, something on par with a Jamie Oliver creation has appeared on your plate.

In fact, watching him cook was better than anything on TV, and I, over the last few months, had forgotten all about it.

I jiggled my wee daughter till she laughed, wondering what he was going to rustle up.

"Who's a delicious girl?" I said as Steven appeared with a tray of dips and a look Nigella Lawson would be proud of.

"Tuck in," he said, sliding a cucumber finger into Baby Bea's mouth.

I watched his small bum as he headed back into the house to investigate Mum's shopping "for inspiration."

As if he needed any.

"What's this?" shouted Steven from the kitchen.

"What?" I shouted back.

"Amongst the courgettes."

"Courgettes?" I said.

"The shopping?" he shouted.

Steven was silent; I could hear rustling, then a Steven chuckle . . .

"Forget it," he shouted. "Just read the note."

And the next thing I knew, Steven was playing the Proclaimers . . .

Chapter Thirty-One

THE PROCLAIMERS

Great sex comes when you least expect.

I had no idea the codpiece was among the fruit and veg, wrapped up like a Christmas present. And I had no idea how it got there. And I still had no idea when Steven put Baby Bea to bed and told me to stay and enjoy the last of the bonfire.

I was on my second glass of wine with a stomach full of delicious food, and we were on the second Proclaimers album. I was thinking of moving on to other music—or, even worse, the TV—when Steven appeared from the kitchen silhouetted by the porch light with the Proclaimers playing my favorite song . . .

I Gonna Be (500miles).

He had nothing on but his boxers, the codpiece, and a look in his eye that took me back ten years—to the hotel where we caused mass destruction in the bathroom.

Something stirred in me, or rather down there. Lust and laughing are so deliciously sexy together, especially when you haven't had any for a long time and have great memories.

Beat—beat—beat—beat . . .

Steven's skinny legs protruding from the giant jeweled codpiece had me in stitches, and yet all I could think about were the times those skinny legs wrapped themselves around me and rocked me senseless.

Steven wiggled his pelvis and the codpiece followed, up and down, side to side; the more he moved, the more it followed. Then he bounced on his heels . . .

Beat—beat—beat—beat . . .

He shimmied his shoulders and twirled a camp twirl, the codpiece following like a brightly colored streamer.

I had never seen the codpiece in all its glory before.

Apart from Helen's gyrating, I had only seen it when Rodger abseiled. And Rodger's abseiling had been a disaster, ending with him crashing to the ground and landing on a wrestler and me being humiliated. It was a night I'd rather forget, a night when my dress caught on Mum's wheelchair and ripped to reveal the worst pair of underpants anyone would want to be seen in—not exactly fun.

Steven looked like he was having fun.

He kicked his leg into the air, followed by some lunges, then jumped up on a stump and swung the codpiece around like a cane.

Beat—beat—beat—beat . . .

Lit up by the moonlight, he swung around the smouldering coals of the fire, twirling his hips. He picked up a stick, tossed it on the fire, grabbed another, twirled it, then, with a *come get me* look, tossed it onto the fire.

"Al fresco dancing," he shouted. "With Rodger's bugle."

There was no one, just us, tree trunks, and the fire goading us to continue . . .

I slipped off my shoes, pressed my feet into the cool damp earth, and stood up; mud squelching between my toes. I swung my hips and let go of every dark feeling in my heart.

I danced about the fire, Steven laughed, and when I saw my chance, I jumped . . .

Steven didn't stand a chance.

The next day, the codpiece lay crumpled by the remains of the bonfire feebly flashing; the batteries were almost done.

Under the flashing light of the codpiece, we made out like teenagers and Baby Bea slept through it all.

The Proclaimers had not even finished their song and I had ripped off the codpiece and anything underneath quicker than a waxing strip.

Then, as the Proclaimers worked their way through every song I could remember, Steven and I worked our way through every position we could remember . . .

"Must have been all that fresh air," laughed Steven.

Baby Bea slept late the next morning, and Steven and I had made the most of it.

By the time Helen had phoned, it was lunchtime. Baby Bea was stirring, and Steven and I, after a couple of rounds of "let's try *it* this way," were ready for something to eat and a rest.

"How was your night?" said Helen.

"We had a fire." I sighed.

"Good night for it," she said. "Al fresco eating and all that?"

I laughed, and before I had a chance to ask about the codpiece, she began talking about Mum's chair.

"I think if the electrics are dried out, it could work again," she said.

Normally I would have been jealous, pissed off, but this morning my mind was on other things, and I felt . . . well . . . knackered.

"Never thought of that." I smiled to Steven.

"Yes, I think I might try a blow-dryer?" she said.

I nodded like she could see me on the phone.

After Helen hung up, I realized I never asked her about the codpiece, despite her telling me the batteries were rechargeable.

I filled the kettle, fingering the note she had left by the codpiece . . .

Knock yourself out, and don't forget to play the Proclaimers. —Helen

"Hidden depths," muttered Steven with a hug.

I twirled the note between my fingers.

"I think I'll wear that blue suit after all."

Chapter Thirty-Two

THE REPORTER

The world's gone mad: part two.

The day before the wedding, I headed to Mum's for a couple of tools. The last few days without visiting had been fantastic, and I wanted to hang on to that feeling for as long as possible, or at least until I had worn and enjoyed the blue suit.

Helen met me by the garage; she was a ball of excitement and apprehension. According to her, Henry was being "an arsehole," sending Amy and Gary into panic mode.

"Why must he be so fucking competitive?" said Helen.

She said "fuck" without any conviction—Amy had turned to her for help, and Helen could not contain her pleasure.

"Competitive?" I said.

She asked if I had seen the local paper.

"Who hasn't . . ." I muttered.

"Well, Henry's pissed."

"Why?"

"It's all about your mum and not him."

I looked at her. "Seriously?"

"Well, he didn't actually say that . . . but he has been going on about weddings and YouTube to Amy . . . and how he had a pal who was good at videoing things, for God's sake."

"I thought Amy wanted it to be a low-key affair."

"After the paper this morning, low key is the last thing Henry is thinking of."

Mum opened the window and began to shout, "Sheryl? Is that you?"

"Oh, and I plonked the paper on your mum's bed as well," said Helen.

"You did what?"

"I gave her the paper," said Helen.

"Jesus! And you're still alive?"

I looked up at the kitchen window. I could see Mum. How many times would she read "feeble," "geriatric," or "elderly" before . . . she'd swear?

Helen laughed. "It had to be done."

"What did she say?" I said, watching Mum's silhouette open the window.

Here we go!

"Sheryl! I can hear you!" she shouted.

"It got her up," said Helen.

I was beginning to see how good Helen was for Mum. Not only had she sorted Mum's wheelchair with a hair dryer, but she stood up to her. Helen's quiet dignity was a perfect match for Mum's dominance. *Giving Mum that article—I would have hidden it.*

The security camera outside Kilmory Headquarters had caught Mum protesting in her wheelchair. The local paper, getting wind of the video, had written an article about the closure of the library and how "the antics of an elderly woman in a wheelchair had plunged the council into a state of panic."

It was written by a has-been reporter who seemed to think that egg boxes were more than "a nod to caged hens and veganism" and that anyone with grey hair was geriatric and anyone who dressed up as a ghost pumpkin had dementia.

"Old woman," Mum shouted from the window. "They are calling me an old woman."

Helen nudged me with an *I knew it would get her going* wink.

We headed up the stairs.

Mum, dressed and angry, was sipping coffee like she hardly noticed it.

"I'm not old. Who are they talking about?" said Mum with a disgusted toss of the paper; it fluttered to the floor.

Helen lifted it. "It's not that bad."

Mum pulled it from her. "She called me a 'pensioner.'"

Helen pulled the paper from her. "Well, you are a pensioner . . ."

Mum sniffed as Helen flicked the paper open and began to read.

"A pensioner has managed to set the council alight with a protest on a scale never seen since the bra-burning days of Germaine Greer."

"Germaine Greer never burnt her bra," said Mum. She caught my eye. "Do you think George has seen this?"

"Everyone has," said Helen.

Mum bit into her toast, her first for days, and talked about suing, humiliation, and how she "couldn't possibly take any more," while Helen continued to read the article over her with the odd look at me.

"'It's a sad state of affairs when the council closes the library due to budget cuts and even sadder that an activist the age of my grandmother is the only one bothered enough to sort things.'"

"You're an activist, Mum," I said.

Mum, now slathering lumps of jam on her toast, stopped. "Activist? This is a good thing?"

She looked from Helen to me.

"So, you think George has read it then?"

Later that day, the article reached the news on Scottish TV.

Steven, Helen, and I gathered around the TV in Mum's house, waiting, mugs poised . . .

The reporter positioned outside the Kilmory offices talked of how a "vegan activist" managed to obstruct the laying of new carpet in the council office's reception before tackling (along with her egg boxes) the local *Indian*."

"That's me," said Mum.

The councilor, a well-fed, well-dressed man, tried to explain the "different budgets for different departments" theory, along with the "use it or lose it" theory.

A theory not lost on a young reporter determined to make a name for herself.

"Are you saying even though you don't need carpets, you, the council, still have to buy them to use up the budget?"

She thrust the microphone into the councilor's face.

"Essentially yes . . . err, no. I mean, that's not quite what I meant," said the councilor.

The reporter's tight blonde hair rustled in the wind. "You're using public money for renovation not required . . . and cutting out audio for the blind?"

"Yes," said Mum with an air punch.

Steven grabbed her not-quite-drunk coffee.

"Audio," said the councilor, "is not *just* for the blind—"

"But you're still cutting it," snapped the reporter.

"—and the carpet is for public use," flustered the councilor.

"Shag pile?" said the reporter with another thrust of her microphone.

"For the last time," snapped the councilor, "the council does not support shag pile."

Two hooded youths sauntered behind and pulled an "up yours" gesture.

"So what *are* you saying?" said the reporter. "That no floors were covered?"

"No, I didn't say that."

"That floor covering is more important than . . . than . . . storytelling to children?"

Mum beamed. "That's me!"

"N-no," stuttered the councilor. "The storytelling is completely irrelevant."

"Are you saying storytelling should be banned?"

"The council has no stance on storytelling," snapped the now red-faced councilor.

"Knobhead! Tosser!" shouted the two hooded youths.

The councilor, with a glare at the two youths, muttered, "This is why budget cuts should be kept top secret . . ."

"Cuts?" said the reporter.

"Did I say 'cuts'? I don't think I did . . ." The councilor attempted a smile.

"You did," said the journalist.

"Give her one," shouted one hooded youth; the other shoved him over.

The councilor's smile dropped as he threw another glare at the youths, who were now in a playful tussle.

"Ma'am, I think you have the . . . err . . . wrong end of the stick."

"Wrong end of the stick? There is no wrong end of the stick, just money being spent on carpets while libraries are being shut *willy-nilly* . . ."

"I never mentioned willies . . ."

The two youths fell about laughing.

"Now you're suggesting it should be top secret?" said the journalist.

"You're taking everything out of context," snapped the councilor.

"That literature should be monitored by the MFI?" said the reporter.

"I think you mean MI5," muttered the councilor.

"Shag piles are for wankers," shouted the youths.

The news desk flashed onto the screen, and as the newsreader began a joke about how "no furniture was hurt in the making of this news," Mum flicked off the TV mid punchline and turned to us.

"Do you think George was watching?"

Helen's phone pinged. "Well, Henry certainly was," said Helen. "He's been on the phone to Amy . . . according to her, he's super pissed."

"So what?" said Steven.

"Yeah, so what?" said Mum.

Helen answered her phone; the noise of a pub blasted her ear as Henry began to shout. "Now she's on bloody TV!"

We all heard.

Helen asked Henry if he had been drinking.

"I'm having a wee beer in Argyll's most famous pub."

"He's in the Comm," muttered Helen.

"Just a quiet pint," said Henry, "celebrating my daughter's *impending* wedding—"

A few cheers from the bar.

"—and *she* appears on the TV."

A few more cheers.

"I said to Brian here, if that woman can get on the TV—"

"She wasn't exactly *on* the TV," said Helen.

"—then my daughter's wedding can get on that YouTube what's-it-thing, and—"

"You tell 'em, Henry!"

"Amy on YouTube?" muttered Mum. "She'd rather have a hot poker up her what's-it-thing."

"—and . . . I have an idea that will give her more hits than Prince Harry's Haka."

Helen looked at me.

"It's a rugby thing," muttered Mum.

"That's right, more hits than Harry Whatshisface," yelled Henry.

"Good enough for Prince Harry . . ."

"Aye, good enough for royalty . . ."

"Jesus," muttered Steven. "How many has he had?"

Henry laughed. "Don't you worry. I said to Amy, 'It's all in hand.'"

"You tell 'em . . ."

"I've an idea that will knock the *friggin'* socks off this town," said Henry.

"Yeah, Henry!"

"Amy doesn't want any socks knocked off," said Helen.

More cheering from the pub.

"And neither does Gary."

"Nothing but the best for our daughter," said Henry to a chorus of applause and hung up.

Steven told her to ignore it. "What can he do now? The wedding's tomorrow, and he'll be hungover—hopefully."

Mum threw me a look. "Exactly."

Chapter Thirty-Three

THE DINNER

There is more to support than a good bra.

It was Henry's idea for Amy and Gary to do a special dance for the wedding, despite the fact that neither were dancers.

Gary's ability to dance was on par with Steven's ability to wrestle . . . and Amy's wasn't much better. They were more comfortable walking up a hill or fishing than dancing. In fact, the whole wedding thing was way out of Amy's "comfort zone," as she put it, and the last thing she felt like doing was trying to tango in a tight white dress in front of Gary's family.

Gary didn't say anything. He had no idea what a tango was; he thought it was a drink and said as much in the Loch Fyne Hotel, where Henry had brought up the whole "special dance" idea months ago.

It was the first time Helen had met Gary's parents, Edna and Ted. The date for Amy and Gary's wedding had been set, and they all decided to meet, celebrate, and "chew over a few wedding ideas."

Helen, still recovering from her parking attendant debacle, asked Steven and I to join.

To be honest, I'd rather have my wrist burnt with a hot poker than go through wedding talk. Steven, however, wanted to support his sister . . .

"So," said Henry, polishing off the last of his smoked salmon, "what song are you going to dance to?" He smiled at his daughter. "Or is that a secret?"

"Dance?" said Gary. He looked at Amy.

"We weren't," said Amy, returning Gary's panicked look.

"But the couple always has the first dance," said Edna.

"Exactly," said Henry.

"Everyone will be expecting it," said Edna.

"Everyone?" said Helen.

"Of course," said Edna. "It's a given."

"I hate dancing," muttered Gary.

Edna patted her now-depressed-looking son's hand. "All's you need is a simple waltz." She gestured to Ted. "If Bozo the Clown over there can, anyone can."

Ted stopped. "If I had a drink for every time you said that, I'd be an alcoholic."

"Waltz?" said Henry. "I was thinking something with a kick to it: salsa, maybe a tango, or Zumba . . ."

Helen and I looked at each other. Was he mad?

Henry pulled out his iPhone and began to flick through YouTube with a "what about this?" to Ted.

"Very Hollywood," muttered Ted.

"It's their wedding," said Helen.

"Exactly," muttered Henry, absorbed.

"Waltz is fine—teachable," said Edna.

"So why are you choosing the song?" said Helen.

Amy, glancing at Henry's phone, flashed a look of horror at her mum.

"We don't want anything big, just something small, casual."

"Small, casual? Not for my daughter—my daughter should have something amazing, earth-shattering." He ruffled his daughter's hair. "Nothing but the best for my daughter," he said.

"Still think a waltz would be easier," muttered Edna. "Or perhaps a mild salsa at a push."

"But he's no dancer," said Ted, gesturing with his knife.

"Don't point," snapped Edna.

"I'll point if I want to," snapped Ted, "I'm paying for this stuff . . ." Ted pushed at his untouched garnish.

Edna threw him a *shut it* look.

"Be better off at the chippie," muttered Ted, "least I'd be full."

"If they want something small, what's wrong with that?" said Steven. "Why spend money on something you don't want?"

"Our wedding was a nightmare to pay off," said Ted. "And I was still hungry afterwards."

"Yes, but it was worth it," snapped Edna.

"Worth it? All that money for a photo album?"

"Well, I for one was glad. One of the few chances I got to dress up."

"I could have built a hotel for that price," muttered Ted.

Edna threw him a look. "What the hell would you do with a hotel?"

"Sell proper food for a start," said Ted with a disgruntled push of his plate.

Amy looked at her father. She patted his hand and told him how much she appreciated his help, "but really, all we want is something small, cozy, just a few friends—a couple of tables, a few laughs, nothing more."

"Nothing more?" said Henry. "I was thinking the presidential suite at the Columba for you."

Amy gaped at her father. "That's huge, takes hundreds." She looked at Gary. "Do we know that many people?"

"Do they really need a big wedding?" said Helen. "I mean, it's not everyone idea of fun, is it?"

"Fun? What's fun got to do with marriage?" said Ted.

"You're just being ridiculous," snapped Edna. "Here, have my drink and shut up."

"We never had much for our wedding," said Helen.

"Neither did we," said Steven.

"Exactly," said Henry.

"We were married in a portacabin," said Helen.

"On the beach," said Steven.

"Sounds like heaven," muttered Ted.

"Exactly," said Henry.

"Followed by scampi and chips," muttered Helen.

"What I wouldn't give for some scampi now," snapped Ted, emptying his glass.

Steven looked at me questioningly.

"Chocolate cake," I said. "You made it."

Steven's face lit up. "Yes . . . delicious."

"No scampi for my daughter, or"—Henry glanced at me—"chocolate cake. My daughter deserves the real thing."

"What are you saying? My chocolate cake was plastic?" said Steven.

"I like that sound of that," said Gary. "Chocolate cake, sand between your toes—no dancing."

"I liked our wedding," muttered Helen, "it was just afterwards . . ."

Henry, not listening, expanded on his ideas for a wedding, and no amount of "but Dad" daunted him. He knew Amy's favorite colors, Gary's favorite foods, and just about every hotel in the area; even I was impressed.

Edna certainly was.

"Wonderful . . . splendid," she muttered as the puddings arrived, while Ted, glumly staring at his "deconstructed" trifle, moaned about the lack of cream.

"At least I'm not paying for the shindig," he muttered, which everyone chose to ignore.

Gary, in silence, sipped his water. I could see him adding up the cost of Henry's suggestions.

"It sounds so expensive," said Amy. "We can't afford anything so . . . extravagant."

"Oh, didn't I tell you? I'm paying," said Henry.

"What?" Elma dropped her fork.

"No," said Steven.

"You can't," said Amy.

"Seriously?" muttered Gary.

"Let me get you a drink," said Ted.

Helen threw me a *fucking hell* look.

"It's not often your only child gets married," exclaimed Henry, pushing the lunch bill towards Ted . . .

Several meetings, phone calls, and texts later, Gary, a Dolly Parton fan, agreed to dance to "Island in the Stream"—bribing the best men and bridesmaids to join in "at the first chorus," even agreeing to a few dancing lessons . . .

And Henry had almost come to terms with it all, until, that is, Mum appeared on Scottish TV . . . and he, with only a photo in the local paper, was cheesed off.

For some reason, it sparked in Henry a ruthless competitiveness not seen by many, except Helen. The father of the bride wanted more; something worthy of YouTube.

Dolly Parton, it seemed, was "old hat."

Chapter Thirty-Four

THE DANCE

A newly married couple's first dance is more eye contact than technique.

On the morning of the wedding, we raced around with hair dryers and irons while Mum watched. Helen was a bundle of nerves, dropping mugs of coffee and snapping at Mum for getting in the way.

Steven tried to calm her down with many "what the hell can Henry do now?" comments, and finally after a large whisky, she stopped swearing and headed over to help her daughter.

The wedding reception was not far from Lochgilphead, right by the canal at the Cairnbaan Hotel.

We met Helen outside the church. I was in my blue suit; Steven, looking handsome in a kilt, was clutching Baby Bea, also in blue, while Helen was wearing an orange lace dress with a navy blue jacket and an impressive "catch any breeze" hat, along with shoes that required half a bottle of whisky to balance in.

It was the sort of outfit that would never see the light of day again and the sort of hat that was so large it doubled up as a very colorful umbrella.

It took Helen about an hour of shopping before she had given up and allowed Mum to take over who ordered, online, the sort of clothes that someone in a wheelchair would have no problems wearing, and someone who never wore heels, let alone a hat would require a decent amount of *anything alcoholic* to feel comfortable in.

"You can't go wrong with lace and velvet," said Mum and Helen ended up looking as she did: nothing like her usual hardworking self, and stunning.

I wanted to hug her, tell her she looked fantastic; instead, Steven handed me Baby Bea and did it, and he was still doing it when Amy arrived.

Henry, looking surprisingly fresh in a kilt and superbly long sporran, walked Amy down the aisle while Helen sat next to her brother, muttering "codpiece" under her breath until she saw her daughter's glowing face . . . and then she stopped as a tear filled her eye.

The wedding service had been a traditional and yet delicious affair, which went, according to Gary, "as smooth as a baby's bum."

The photos took forever, the meal went down without a hitch, and the speeches . . . well, what can I say?

Henry stood to cheering on par with a football pitch, recognized as "he who saved the storyteller." He basked in the moment, milking the applause without mentioning Helen once.

Amy didn't clap; neither did Gary.

"Nothing but the best for my daughter," he finally toasted as the waiter topped up our drinks.

People began to look expectantly at the stage. Henry had promised something special in his speech, which had the rest of the wedding party a little on edge, apart from Helen; she was looking as comfortable as she did working on a roof (her favorite place to relax).

She and Henry were getting on like a house on fire, at times looking like a happily married couple.

Henry had been plying her with drinks.

"It's all good," said Helen, pulling up a seat. She slipped off her hat as we watched Henry work the room. He caught Helen's eye and winked.

Helen chuckled.

"What's up with him?" I said.

"God knows," tutted Steven.

"You and me," Henry mouthed to Helen, "so proud of our daughter," then sent another drink Helen's way.

Helen nodded with a smile.

"It seems the 'knock their socks off' comment was just a drunken promise," she sighed with a long sip of her drink.

Henry waved at her; she waved back.

"Just the dances now," muttered Helen.

Helen followed me to the ladies' looking the happiest I seen her in ages. It was empty apart from a buxom-looking woman applying lipstick with two-bottles-of-Prosecco precision.

Helen looked at herself in the mirror. "I'm beginning to wonder about heels and hats. Do you think it would have made a difference?" she said.

"Difference to what?" I said.

"Our marriage," she said. "Perhaps if I had made an effort, dressed up more?"

I threw her a *you are joking* look.

"I mean, we did have a daughter together," said Helen.

"It's the wedding," said Ms Buxom with a smack of her lips. "Always brings exes together."

"Aye," said a voice from the toilet.

"Together?" muttered Helen.

Ms Buxom eyed Helen. "That Henry—he is your ex, I take it?"

"Well, yes," said Helen.

Ms Buxom pulled a face. "Arsehole of a speech."

"Totally," yelled the voice from the toilet.

"It's supposed to be about your daughter, not him," said Ms Buxom.

"That's what I said," said the voice from the toilet.

Helen looked confused.

Ms Buxom pulled out a mascara. "Take it from me," she said.

"Aye, take it from her," said the voice over the flush of the toilet. "She's an expert."

Ms Buxom threw a glare at the toilet door.

The toilet door clicked open and a blonde appeared. She flashed a smile at Helen and me, staggered to the washbasin, and gestured to Ms

Buxom. "*She* went weak at the knees when she saw *her* ex at a wedding."

The Blonde thrust her hands under the tap. "Next thing she's in the back of his car, heels in the air like a sixteen-year-old giving birth."

"They don't want to hear about *that*," snapped Ms Buxom.

"Totally smitten," said the Blonde with a flick of the paper towel.

"Aye, all right," said Ms Buxom.

"One glass of Prosecco," said the Blonde, slapping lipstick on like sun cream, "and she's a friggin' horse to be ridden."

"I told you, it was more than a glass, and it was just the once, all right?" said Ms Buxom.

"All he had to do was crook his finger . . ." The blonde laughed with a smack of her lips.

"Yes . . . well . . . we all make mistakes," said Ms Buxom, wrenching the lipstick from the Blonde's hand.

The Blonde skidded.

Ms Buxom steadied her friend and with a "mind" and marched her to the door; she glanced back at Helen.

"The trick is not to make the same mistake," she said.

"Same mistake?" laughed the Blonde. "Who are you kidding? You can't stop making *the* same mistake."

Ms Buxom pushed her out the door.

"Who was that?" I said.

"No idea," said Helen, "but there's no way I'm ending up in the back of Henry's sports car; putting the seat belt on in that thing is hard enough, let alone any tongue gymnastics."

We headed back to Steven at the table. The bar was full, and right at the front were Ms Buxom and the Blonde cracking jokes with Henry—he was buying the drinks.

I was about to make a joke about cocktails, sport cars, and three-somes when the band began to warm up their guitars.

"Ten minutes to the bride's first dance," mumbled one of the guitarists, glancing at the unattended drums.

Edna, with an *I've got something you're not going to like* look, pulled up a chair beside Helen and launched into a story of Henry that stopped Steven in his tracks and had Helen choking on her Spumante.

Chapter Thirty-Five

THE WEDDING

Shit sex has nothing to do with coming.

"You have no idea what an idiot he is," said Edna.

"Think we do," I muttered.

Edna threw Helen a look. "He's going to do something . . . ballroom-y . . . strictly ballroom-y."

"Henry?" said Steven.

"Latin ballroom-y . . ." said Edna.

"Aye right," said Steven. "He is as much into Latin as Sheryl's mum's into chanting."

"He listens to it in the car," said Edna.

"He does not," said Helen.

"He does too," said Edna.

"The only thing he listens to in the car is gear changes," snapped Helen. "That man has as much time for music as he did me."

"He is completely addicted to it," said Edna. "He says it 'makes the grey wet days almost bearable.'"

"I find that as believable as your Ted doing a lap dance," said Steven.

Edna blushed.

The guitarist tapped the microphone. "Make that twenty minutes," he said, glancing at the empty drums.

Edna sipped her bubbly and talked of how she and Henry shared a love of music, dancing, and the heat of Latin America.

"He just loves to drill to a tango . . . tinker to a salsa." She sighed.

We looked at her with disbelief.

"Henry never tinkered," muttered Helen. "Not even on our honeymoon."

Edna eyed Helen. "Apparently, it helped him cope with the split."

"Good for him." Steven tilted his glass.

"He wants his moment in front of an audience . . ." said Edna.

"What are you, his best buddy?" said Helen.

"I'm a dance teacher," sniffed Edna.

"Forgot about that," muttered Helen.

"And he's gonna dance," said Edna.

Helen choked on her wine. "Dance! He can't even shuffle—he is as musical as a bulldog. He wouldn't know a two-step from a nosebleed."

Steven looked at his sister. "How much have you had to drink?"

"I taught him," said Edna, "and he sort of got carried away."

"For fuck's sake," said Helen.

Edna shifted uncomfortably. "He just wanted to impress his daughter. He said he had a lot to make up for. He said he never thought he could dance, and I"—she gulped her wine—"stupidly told him anyone could learn, except of course that bozo husband of mine."

She sighed. "The men I have taught."

I watched her sipping her drink, lost in (I presume) distant memories of men, music, and Latin moves.

She flashed a look at me. "Then *your* mother made it—big time."

"Big time?" I said.

"And he was *livid*."

"He's always livid," Steven and Helen said together.

"Thanks to your Mum, he has spent a week digesting every stupid wedding dance on YouTube . . ."

"Thanks to *my* Mum?" I said.

The two young guitarists looked at the unattended drum kit. One pulled out his phone.

"Where the fuck are you?" he hissed.

"He's come up with a plan," said Edna. "A stupid plan . . . a rock-of-all-ages montage dance plan . . ."

"That's original," muttered Steven.

"I told him, 'Henry,' I said, ' I don't think your daughter's wedding is your moment.' But would he listen?"

"He did mention sock rocking . . ." muttered Steven.

"'A smooth waltz is all that's required,' I said. And do you know what he said?"

"'Nothing but the best for my daughter,'" muttered Helen.

Edna gestured us closer.

"He's brought a sporran the length of a cricket bat."

"Shit," said Helen.

"I can't stop thinking about it—my poor Gary. The last thing he needs is that twat and his cricket-bat sporran ruining the day."

Henry looked at Helen and gave her another wink.

"So that's why he's only on tonic water," muttered Helen.

The two guitarists minus a drummer played "Islands in the Stream" as Amy and Gary took to the floor for their first dance.

Amy and Gary gazed at each other like there was no one else in the room. They laughed; he kissed her head as she slid her arms around his neck . . .

As the song was on the last chorus Gary ushered the best men and the bridesmaids onto the floor; there were hugs, kisses, and overenthusiastic singing as all in the room swayed to the music.

It almost made me want to get married again.

Henry took Edna and twirled like a professional, while Helen and Ted raced about like they wanted the dance to end.

Once the song was finished, Henry grabbed the microphone and talked of his daughter as a DJ as ancient as my mother's kitchen appeared. When he moved on to the dad-and-daughter's dance, Helen looked at me.

"But we don't do traditional here," he said.

"Shit," muttered Steven.

Chapter Thirty-Six

THE COMM

A good entrance is nothing without an audience.

Mum had spent the night before claiming how glad she was that she wasn't coming, as the last thing she wanted to do was "upstage the bride."

"Who needs an activist at a wedding, especially a vegan one," she said more than once.

Like an egg had never touched her lips.

We should have guessed, taken more notice, when, after flicking the TV off, she spent the rest of the evening wheeling about her room organizing an outfit for the "pensioners shopping day" in Stirling. *Like that was for real.*

Turns out there was no shopping trip, but there were several texts from Francis about George and what he was up to.

He'd been seen at the Comm . . . along with Tunie, the man with the largest boat in the Ardrishaig Basin.

Henry had arranged for his great pal Tunie to sail Amy to the church and both Amy and Gary from the church to the hotel along the canal. Tunie, often referred to as the "Moby Dick of the Canal" (from those who'd never read the book), had the sailing skills of an admiral and the patter of Para Handy and looked pretty good in a kilt. But he was strictly a one-pint-a-day man and, thanks to Henry, ended up with his head over a toilet, "spewing," to quote the barman, "his ringer."

Henry took one look at a cross-eyed Tunie, who was shouting "It will be all right on the night" at a urinal, and called the only man he knew who could get Tunie home; George.

"You need to look after him," said Henry, "and make sure Amy gets to the church."

George, who by now had turned up at his sister's house vowing never to set foot near "that Hound of the Bastilles Beatrice again," at first said "no."

"I am still incognito," he shouted down the phone.

Like a half-cut Henry would understand . . .

His sister told him not to be so stupid, reminded him what friendship was all about, and said that Tunie's boat was a handy thing to have the use of, and when that didn't work, she swore blind the last person to be at that wedding was Beatrice, who according to her was "also still *incognito.*"

George appeared, dragged Tunie to his boat, and settled him in.

"She'll be all right on the night," shouted Tunie several times before hurling his fish supper, along with several pickled eggs, into the canal.

The next day, hungover, with flatulence that would spark a bonfire and an upset stomach that required spare underpants, Tunie asked George to step in.

Sipping a weak sugary tea, he feebly lifted his head and looked at his pal.

"Save the wedding," he muttered.

To quote George, "What choice did I have?"

With no time to go home, he slipped into Tunie's kilt and took the helm, sailing Amy up the canal while Tunie dozed below mumbling incoherently.

"Never again a pickled egg . . ."

Francis, whose son owned the hotel, was supposedly helping. She spotted George at the helm miles away and texted Mum, "Guess who's here in a way-too-tight kilt?" shortly followed by a picture of George helping Amy out of the boat . . .

None of us noticed George; we were too busy tucking into the vol-au-vents and bubbly to notice. We thought they were still having their photos taken.

It was Francis, clutching a tray of empty glasses, who pointed it out. She pulled me aside . . .

"Guess who's here?" she said.

"Who?" I said.

"George," she said.

Steven choked on his orange squash. "George? I thought he'd fallen off the planet."

"Where?" I said.

"He's driving the boat," said Francis.

"Sail, darling," said a passerby.

"What boat?" said Steven.

Francis, pointing with a limp beer mat, said, "That boat."

"For Chrissake, don't tell Beatrice," said Helen.

"Oh . . ." Francis blushed and swiftly left to clear a table.

Mum claimed she only kept in touch with Francis to see what everybody was wearing. The last thing she intended to do was, well . . . what she ended up doing.

As she said later, "Seeing George in a kilt helping Amy out of Tunie's boat was almost too much, but when Francis followed it up with pictures of George tucking into a prawn vol-au-vent . . . it was like the angels up above spoke to me. 'Grab your chance, Beatrice,' they said, and I did. *Thank God I was prepared . . .*"

Three phone calls and a bribe for God-knows-what later, Mum, thanks to a volunteer driver, was being wheeled into the ballroom, while Henry was supposedly "rocking the socks off" Lochgilphead.

To give Mum her due, she did try to sneak in, but as Francis pointed out later, "A wheelchair whirling onto a dance floor is enough to capture anyone's attention, and when driven by Beatrice, 'the talk o' the steamie' . . . even the splits couldn't compete with that."

Chapter Thirty-Seven

THE PELVIS AND ELVIS

Get my lipstick, open the malt; we have a wedding to get to.

Henry had a pelvis of epic flexibility—a pelvis that made Elvis Presley look like a stick insect—and as he ripped off his kilt in the middle of the dance floor, the room fell silent.

No one was prepared for what was underneath . . .

Henry, a man way past his best with the slim legs of Mr Bean and looking nothing like John Travolta, pulled a *Saturday Night Fever* pose—minus the white suit.

The band stopped and the crowd hushed as they stared at a Lycra kilt so tightly stretched across Henry's hips that *all* underneath was visible.

Henry had gone commando, his modesty precariously covered by a sporran suspended like a giant upside-down fox tail, and it swung too freely for my liking.

Henry, a man old enough to have grandchildren, had chosen to "swing freely" in a room full of grannies (who'd seen it all and weren't fussed about seeing it again) and children (who had no idea about such things as pubic hair)—and he had chosen to do it to Black Magic Woman by Santana, a band nobody in Scotland under the age of sixty had heard of and a song as old fashioned as flares.

"Jesus," muttered Steven, along with pretty much everyone in the room.

"What the fuck?" slurred the young man at the next table.

The DJ, doddery and (judging by the volume) deaf, fumbled behind his equipment.

Someone yelled, "Turn it down."

The DJ nodded an *okay* and turned it up, causing a few toddlers to cry and Amy's granny to rip out her hearing aid in disgust.

God knows what Henry had planned, but if it was anything like his music, it was a blessing that Mum turned up when she did. The music was as appropriate for Amy's wedding as Henry's sporran, not to mention the *jump*.

Henry started with a twist, his swishing sporran giving away way too much of his manhood for my liking and, from the look on her face, Amy's too. Then he bounced into a squat and struggled to get up.

"Are we meant to be laughing?" muttered a passing waiter.

Helen, whose emotions, to quote her, had been "on a roller coaster," shook her head with a *no idea* . . . until she, along with the children, spied Mum entering.

Tunie, who it seemed did know Santana, was merrily pushing Mum into the ballroom with no idea who was dancing . . .

He had, according to him, come across Mum struggling to wheel herself up the steps into the hotel, and he did "what any decent fella would do"; pushed. And he kept pushing until he, inches from the dance floor, caught sight of his mate making the sort of moves any six-year-old would be ashamed of.

Tunie skidded to a stop just shy of the dance floor.

"Jesus," he mouthed as the wheelchair slipped from his hands.

Mum's wheelchair, not quite resurrected to its former glory, continued to roll . . .

The crowd gasped and the children pointed as Mum, done up like a Christmas cracker, appeared through the fog of the smoke machine, stopping under flashing disco lights.

She looked stunned.

"Very Ricky Gervais," muttered a waiter.

Mum had on her "I'm not going down without a fight" outfit that she wore to impress her sister (though nothing impressed her); she claimed it was "never in fashion, so it will never go out." An outfit she bought from a dubious-looking Ann Summers lookalike shop that had her crashing into the vibrators with a gay abandonment that had me shrinking in my shoes. An outfit of orange leather, yellow lace ruffles, and a hat that Captain Jack Sparrow would be proud of.

Steven called it her "Pirates of the Caribbean look."

"It's the storyteller," yelled a wee one.

"What the hell has she got on?" muttered Amy's gran.

"I thought I'd never see that again," muttered Steven.

To be fair, there had been a lot of alcohol drunk.

Henry did his best to carry on with grim determination as the crowd, finally recognizing Mum as "the vegan activist on YouTube," began to cheer with a *what's going to happen next?* expectancy.

Santana's guitars blasted into the air, and Henry, taking his cue from the riff, did what any decent narcissist would do . . .

He went for the jump.

Henry propelled himself into the air like a stuntman out of an explosion . . .

The crowd hushed . . . as he collapsed into a half-hearted cartwheel.

Mothers covered their children's eyes as Henry's family jewels briefly flashed under the pulsating lights, and before there was time to work out what size it was, he skidded into the splits.

A few winced, including Henry, as the DJ, who I suspected needed glasses, turned up the volume yet again.

Something got into Mum. Maybe it was George watching on the sidelines, the flashing disco lights bringing back memories, or her outrageous outfit, or maybe she just happened to like Santana—who knows. But Mum, rising like a phoenix from the ashes, took to the floor like a pro any disabled person would be proud of.

She, with a jaunty tilting of her hat, swirled her wheelchair backwards, then forwards, then *hung a wheelie.*

The crowd stared; the children shouted for more.

Henry, still wincing on the floor, glared . . .

George, clutching a whisky, appeared beside me as Mum continued to circle the floor to a crescendo of drums and guitars as foreign to the crowd as Henry's get-up.

George laughed. "Only she could get away with *that* and *that* get-up."

Mum's timely moves had most of us forgetting our drinks. She hit each beat with a twist, a turn, a flick of her hat, until after one final wheelie, she tossed the hat into the crowd, pulled Henry onto her knee, and wheeled him off.

"Thank fuck for that woman," muttered Amy's gran before dropping off to sleep.

Francis, acting as receptionist, waitress, and general dogsbody, ushered Mum and Henry to a quiet corner behind the reception desk, dramatically clearing a couch of papers.

I, along with Edna, Ted, and Tunie, watched Henry ease himself onto the couch like a war hero.

"Bloody fool," snapped Ted, checking for any broken bits.

Henry dramatically winced in pain as he spread his legs out on the couch like a starfish, his Lycra hiding little.

"I told him," muttered Edna. "'Jumping takes months of practice,' I said, but would he listen? 'I haven't months,' that's what he said."

Henry let out a loud moan.

Edna threw a look at him. "'Months for what?' I said."

"Whisky," moaned Henry, "any whisky?"

"I wanted to do something sweet," she said. "Wainwright, the Temptations, perhaps some Stevie Wonder, finishing off with a smooth James Taylor . . ."

She gestured towards the apparition of Henry. "None of this jump-and-splits malarkey. 'Tradition,' I told him, 'you can't beat tradition.' I mean, it's traditional for a reason . . ."

"Some pelvises are just not meant to be seen in public," muttered Francis, tossing a blanket over Henry's "bits."

Mum, puffed and looking happier than I'd seen her in years,

laughed. "That was fantastic, right off the cuff. I had them in the palm of my hand." She looked at me. "Didn't I?"

"I need a drink," groaned Henry.

"Should we call an ambulance?" muttered Francis.

"Nah," said Tunie, handing his pal a large whisky. "He's a tough ol' boot."

"I had no idea he was so flexible," muttered Edna.

"Me neither," muttered Francis.

Henry sipped his whisky like it was medicine. "There's plenty more where that came from."

"Oh, for Chrissake," muttered Ted.

Mum looked around. "Did I see George?"

Chapter Thirty-Eight

RESURRECTION

A hero's welcome is transient.

The band, taking its cue from Henry's departure, played a few songs and then took a break. The drummer had finally appeared, and Helen, with the aid of coffee, was helping him sober up.

As people left the ballroom for fresh air and a smoke, they caught sight of Mum on the other side of the reception desk talking of "going back in."

Many stopped, some insisting on a selfie.

"You are a hero," said one.

"Giving hope," said another.

"And comedy," said the waiter.

Mum, basking in the attention like an author at her first signing, didn't see George appear . . .

I was discreetly feeding Baby Bea at the time, blissfully watching the world go by and enjoying being left to "get on with it" as George slid Mum's favorite whisky by Francis's side.

"For the hero of the hour," he said, watching Mum embrace her five minutes of fame with the modesty of a five-year-old.

Soon, Ted and Edna, with an *I've had enough* look, left, Ted mumbling about "one last dance before the band packs up" and Edna unable to hide her surprise.

"Seriously, us dancing?" she said.

"Well, if that bozo can, anyone can," muttered Ted.

Henry didn't seem to hear; he had quieten down and stopped the dramatic wincing and moaning in pain. Ms Buxom and the Blonde had appeared with an "oh my God" and were hanging on to his hands like he was on his "last legs."

Ms Buxom was working her way through a packet of wet wipes, mopping Henry's brow while the Blonde was dolling them out.

"Any permanent damage . . . to . . . err, things?" the Blonde asked more than once, like one of us would know.

Henry said nothing, occasionally smirking with a "no worries in that department" whisper.

He seemed soothed, almost comatose, until Amy's gran appeared.

"God bless you, Beatrice," she shouted with a caustic look in Henry's direction. "And we've got you on video."

Henry sprung up. "Video?"

"You can watch it anytime," said Amy's gran.

"If it wasn't for me, there would be nothing to video," hissed Henry.

"Amy's got a link or something," said Amy's gran.

"I was upstaged," said Henry.

"Upstaged?" George threw a look at me.

"I said I was upstaged," Henry yelled at Amy's gran.

"Upstaged?" Amy's gran yelled back. "I call it *rescued*. If it wasn't for this heroic woman here"—Amy's gran gestured with her stick—"*your* daughter wouldn't be talking to you."

"She saved your arse," said Tunie bluntly.

"My arse didn't need saving," shouted Henry.

"Aye right, and I'm a well-done hamburger," shouted Amy's gran.

"Amy was almost in tears," said Francis, "until Beatrice came on."

"Amy?" said Henry. "My Amy? In tears?"

"There, there," muttered Ms Buxom as the Blonde pulled another wet wipe from her bag with a "here."

"Better find her," said Henry, looking from Ms Buxom to the Blonde.

"Probably best to leave her at the moment," muttered Ms Buxom.

"Yeah, she's pretty angry at you," snapped Francis.

"Amy? Angry?" said Henry.

"You nearly ruined her wedding. I'd be buying Beatrice a drink," said Tunie.

"And I'd go easy on yours," muttered Francis.

"I just wanted . . ." Henry flopped back onto his back.

"What?" said the Blonde.

"Her to like me . . ." said Henry.

Mum's cackle rang through the air.

"Like she likes . . . her mum . . ." said Henry.

"Aww, that's so sweet." The Blonde looked at Ms Buxom.

"To please her, show her something," said Henry.

"You showed her something all right," said Tunie. "You showed her what a tit you are."

"Helen was always the good cop, me the bad cop." He feigned a smile at his two women. "I was working, hard—real hard—earning money."

"Cheers," laughed Mum.

"I just wanted a moment," said Henry. "Is that too much to ask?"

"After that performance, a *moment* is as possible as Beatrice doing a tap dance," said George.

Mum cackled.

"But I spent a fortune on this wedding," said Henry. "Doesn't that count?"

"Have a whisky," said Tunie.

"Best to wait," said Ms Buxom.

"Yes, timing." The Blonde patted his hand. "It's all about timing."

It was George who finally took Henry home. After several attempts to catch Mum's attention, George gave up, grabbed Henry under his arm, and, with Tunie on the other side, took him home.

By the time Mum had discovered the whisky George had left, there was no one in reception except for me watching Baby Bea sleep and the resident cat purring beside me.

Amy and Gary had left, the band were playing their last song, and most had gone home, apart from the odd stragglers propping up the bar or asking for just one more "Auld Lang Syne."

"Is he coming back?" she said, wheeling herself about the reception.

"He never said," I said. "But why don't you ring him?"

Mum didn't answer instead she talked of "ending on a high, leave 'em wanting more."

I looked about the dregs of the wedding and, taking the hint, took her home.

Next day I arrived to see Helen looking out of the Mum's kitchen window looking pensive.

She waved, and I headed to the kitchen.

Mum had told Helen about Henry's conversation the night before.

"Good cop, bad cop? How many whiskies had he had?" said Helen.

"That man is jealous of you," said Mum.

"Jealous of me?" said Helen.

"He meant every word," said Mum, "didn't he, Sheryl?"

Helen looked at me; I shrugged. "He did seem . . . remorseful?"

Helen stared for a bit like she was trying to take it all in.

"Never in a million years would I have thought . . ." She paused over her coffee. "I just assumed I annoyed him, that . . . well . . . he hated me."

"He probably does," said Mum flippantly, "but the jealousy is an underlying factor—root cause."

"What are you on about?" I said.

"He wants what she has," said Mum.

I threw her a look.

"Just a guess-like."

"I was always so scared of him," muttered Helen, staring at her coffee.

"But people like you—Helen," said Mum. "No one thinks about

blokes fixing things, they just moan about the mess. But you, you fix like a man, then tidy up like a woman. Now that's impressive."

"What about me? I tidy up," I said.

"And you're a great mother, everyone can see that," said Mum.

"What about me and Baby Bea?" I said.

"So cool and calm," muttered Mum.

I watched Mum finish her coffee and gave up. Expecting a compliment from her was like expecting a heat wave at Christmas time.

"Has anyone seen George?" she said.

Neither of us answered.

"Heard from him?" said Mum.

"No," said Helen and me in unison.

"Bugger," muttered Mum, wheeling to her room.

"Why don't you just ring him?" I said to her back.

"I'm fine, who needs him?" said Mum.

"But you're not fine. George did a lot for you," I said.

I missed him . . . he made life easier.

"Well, he's not here, so I'll just carry on," said Mum.

"Mum, don't be so stubborn."

I really missed his help.

"He's a turncoat," said Mum, posed at her bedroom door.

"Turncoat?" I said, rolling my eyes at Helen.

"Yes. He should ring me—*he* left me at the wedding."

Helen washed her empty mug under the tap and, with a robust shake, muttered, "All that time I wasted smashing things, swearing, and yelling."

"Aye, a lot of time is wasted on that sort of thing. No point being stubborn," said Mum.

"Like you would know," I said to Mum.

"What a waste of anger," muttered Helen.

"No point holding on to that sort of thing," said Mum.

"He ended up making a tit of himself anyway," said Helen.

"Once a tit, always a tit," yelled Mum, heading into her bedroom.

"Exactly," I yelled at Mum's back.

Chapter Thirty-Nine

MAKING UP

Recovery and resurrection are not always the same thing.

It took weeks for Mum to return to normal and even longer for Henry to appear in public again, despite the attentions of Ms Buxom and the Blonde, who, according to Tunie, had been seen driving to and from his place "done up to the nines."

Mum revamped her wardrobe to orange and wore it all the time, parading about like someone famous until folk forgot and reverted to treating her as Beatrice, a crusty old woman in a wheelchair again.

She began to talk of contacting the paper, writing in the comments page about the library and the need for storytellers.

Maybe even resurrect the petition.

And before I had time to ask her how she was going to do this without George's help, one of the committee members from the community centre contacted her regarding the walls of gratitude. She had seen the pictures of Beatrice on YouTube, and those on the committee had an idea.

Mum, high on talk of being needed, insisted on a visit to the co-op.

"I want to celebrate with a decent whisky," she said.

Normally it would have been George who took her.

I helped Mum onto the co-op carpark. She, like a kid on a new bike, zoomed into the chilly winter wind, stopping at the entrance to the co-op.

The doors flashed open, greeting us with George clutching a loaf of bread, slotting coins into a red Poppy Appeal can.

The woman jiggling the tin laughed a "thank you."

Mum stopped.

George stared at her.

Their eyes locked.

"You got a few coins to spare?" The woman rattled her tin at Mum.

"Sheryl? Any change?" said Mum, her eyes still locked with George.

I pulled out a few coins.

Mum began to smile.

George nodded.

"Chubby was right," she said to George.

"Right?" said George.

"About you coming to the wedding."

"It was *very* last minute," said George.

"So, Chubby was right then," said Mum.

"Well, strictly speaking, no, it wasn't like it was planned."

A red-haired woman of similar age to Mum appeared.

She slid a block of cheese into George's hand. "He's hopeless with shopping." She smiled at Mum.

"Oh," said Mum.

I didn't know what to say . . .

She stretched out her hand to Mum. "I saw you at the wedding, my name's Rebecca. You were stunning at the wedding, wasn't she, George?"

He nodded.

"My mother was in a wheelchair. She hardly left the house, and there you were . . ."

"Beatrice is a one-off," muttered the tin rattler. She shook her tin at a passerby.

"George says you play cards," said Rebecca.

"Well, I haven't for a while," said Mum.

"Neither has he," she said, "have you, George?"

"What?" said George.

"I said you haven't played cards for a while."

"Oh that," he muttered.

"I told him he should keep it up, phone his partner, but who listens to your cousin?" Rebecca smiled again.

"Cousin?" said Mum.

"Hmmm." Rebecca nodded. She turned to George. "You miss cards, don't you George?"

"Yes . . . well . . . yes, I do." He looked at Mum. "Definitely I do."

"Me too," muttered Mum.

Silence . . .

The door swished open.

Two children ran in.

The tin rattler shivered as she jiggled the tin at the mother; the mother looked away and carried on inside.

"So, George, what time are you picking Mum up then?" I said.

George looked at Mum. She fluttered her eyes girlishly.

"The usual?" he asked.

Mum nodded with a large smile.

"Excellent," said George with a large smile back.

That afternoon, in the co-op, Mum bought not only her favorite whisky but a selection of George's favorite cheese *and* a spare toothbrush, and as she lined them up at the checkout, I said nothing.

I knew better.

Helen, having struck up a rapport with the drummer at the wedding, was excited. While sobering him up, they had talked of drumming. He was an ancient man who had played drums all his life.

"He used to teach," said Helen, "years ago, but he couldn't remember the last time someone had bothered to listen to him, let alone ask him to teach. In fact," she said, "he seemed to brighten up at the prospect, even set a date . . ."

"He was drunk at the time," I said.

"He said he is going to start with the basics on a cajon," said Helen.

I threw her a look.

"We've had a few lessons, he says I am a natural." She looked at me. "I could play when you belly dance."

I told her I hadn't done any for a while and the classes seemed to have "fallen by the wayside."

"You should get Neff to start up again. Imagine learning with drums," said Helen.

The thought did appeal.

We arranged to meet Neff in the Stables coffee shop to talk about drumming and dancing. Neff seemed excited. In fact, she was so excited she was there at the table waiting for us, telling the waitress all about the new classes. The waitress had all the time in the world; the cafe was empty apart from a young couple just finishing in the corner, and the cook was reading the paper.

"You should come, it works wonders for the pelvis," said Neff as I pulled up a seat and Helen went to the ladies.

I was just in the middle of ordering coffee when the Blonde and Ms Buxom appeared and stood at the counter, staring at the menu like they had never seen it before; apparently, they were as welcome at Henry's aunt's café as Helen.

They were ordering a takeaway, rolls, and sausage, and as they argued over tomato or brown sauce, Neff called them over.

Neff, who knew them as Janice and Janet, seemed to be on best-buddy terms as they greeted her with a hug.

"Fancy joining us for some belly dancing?" she said. "We are thinking of starting up again with drums this time."

Janet and Janice didn't answer; instead, spotting Helen appearing from the ladies, they grabbed her and launched into a monologue of how Henry was "a broken man."

"Broken man how?" said Helen.

"His daughter won't answer his calls, says he ruined her wedding."

"I see," muttered Helen, pulling up a chair.

"Can you speak to Amy?" said Janice.

"Yes, give the poor guy another chance," said Janet.

Helen stared at the menu, saying little.

"He'll get over it," I said. "A man like him always does, he's ruthless."

"I'm sure you can help." Janice looked at Helen.

Helen remained silent.

"You know you want to," muttered Janet.

Helen continued to stare at the menu. "I'm not sure I can." She slid the menu aside and looked at the two women. "I mean, Amy is her own person."

"She is kind though," I said.

"That's true," said Helen. She let out a long sigh. "She'll probably come around. Just give her time. Seeing your father in a Lycra kilt is not something you can easily forget."

"A kilt, in Lycra?" said the waitress.

"He feels like an idiot," muttered Janet, brushing her blonde hair from her eyes.

"We've known him for years," said Janice. "Never seen him like this before."

"Never heard of a kilt in Lycra," said the waitress.

"Well, neither did we until we saw it," muttered Janice.

"But wouldn't it stick to things?" said the waitress.

"Like cling film," said Helen.

The couple in the corner chuckled.

"Except of course when you cartwheel," I said.

The waitress's eyes widened. "He cartwheeled in it?"

"Like a starfish," I said.

The cafe erupted; even Janet and Janice laughed.

"If only he were trying to be funny," said Janice.

"And it hadn't been at a wedding," said Janet.

"And he'd worn knickers," I said.

"Jesus," muttered the waitress, "the poor daughter."

After Janet and Janice left, Helen started to laugh, then ordered a large cream cake. "I am in the mood for something delicious," she said.

According to Neff, Janice and Janet knew Henry from the Comm; they worked there, and Henry was a regular. He fixed almost everything in the place and always, according to Neff, with a joke, "drain-pipes and lubricant being his favorite."

I hadn't been to the Comm in years; in fact, I can't remember when. Probably back in the days when there were only four channels on TV, pubs had darts matches instead of Sky, and cigarettes were as cheap as crisps.

"The good old days," laughed Neff, pulling out her mobile to text Mavis about the drums. "She'll be wet with excitement."

The waitress, pulling a disgusted face, shouted "Three Americanos" at the kitchen door and, with another "Jesus," headed back into the kitchen.

Chapter Forty

VISITORS

Contentment has a price—lackluster on par with TV dinners in front of TV reruns.

Helen and I had just finished for the day when Mum texted: "Where are you?"

Like I had arranged to meet her.

Which was quickly followed by "They are here, come now."

Like I knew what she was talking about.

I looked at Helen unpacking the van in the garage. "Were we–I to meet her or something?" I said.

Helen stopped mid extension lead rolling. "No, I was just about to put my feet up. Last thing I feel like is—"

She stopped; her mobile pinged.

She dropped the extension lead, pulled out her mobile, and read out loud . . .

"'You too, the more the safer.'"

She looked at me. "Amy's coming around. It's the first time I've seen her since the wedding." She stopped. "Why don't you come up after you've seen your Mum? Amy's bringing wine left over from the wedding."

I didn't say anything. The last thing I wanted after a Mum visit was to sit in Helen's heap of a home trying to find space to put my feet up

—not my idea of fun no matter how many wines. I mean, even Mum refused to go there . . .

I was about to put up a fight when Helen's mobile pinged again; she looked down at it and read out a text from *Mum*. "'Bring Amy as well . . .'"

Helen looked at me with a *how did she know?* look.

"Mother sees all!" I said with a spooky face.

Helen's phoned pinged again. She looked at it, smiled, then flashed her phone at me.

I stared at a row of emoji smiley faces.

"I thought Steven is the only one privileged with those," I said.

Helen laughed.

We headed up to Mum's, and she greeted us at the door and ushered us in with a "*they* are here."

Still in our work clothes, we reluctantly followed to find that *they* was a tight-faced retired army woman, "rank unknown."

I recognized the face and so did Helen; we had recently fitted her kitchen. In fact, her kitchen was the first job Helen and I had worked on together.

She was a woman not to be argued with, a woman with a stiff upper lip and an ability to knock a bill to half and never stop talking to take a breath. We had been warned by many: Mum's pal Mavis being one, Neff being another, and George.

"Go in high," he said. "She'll knock the bill by half at least. And she'll talk you into submission. Once her mouth opens, it never shuts —a tsunami of words."

It was also the job that had bonded Helen and me.

We spent several hours in Mum's kitchen going over the plans while Mum ranted on about the "ridiculous size of kitchens these days," the "pointlessness of islands in kitchens," and why anyone needed "multiple ovens and walk-in freezers when the co-op, Pizza Hut, and any other takeaway she could think of was just two steps away."

Not that I knew anyone who had a walk-in freezer, let alone a Pizza Hut nearby, but Mum was prone to exaggerations. And her exaggerations cheered both Helen and I up as we tried to plan, price, and outwit a penny-pinching ex-army hero with more medals on her wall than my gran's plate collection, one being pinned on her chest by the Queen, which we heard about ad infinitum. In fact, Helen and I had perfected the art of sign language while hammering, drilling, plastering, and feigning listening: builders' multitasking that only two women in sync could perfect.

"How's your new kitchen?" said Mum.

She eyed Mum's wheelchair. "You can call me Ms Frasier."

"Well then, Ms Frasier, can you tell these two your plans?"

Ms Frasier's eyes ran up and down our outfits, taking in the splattered jeans and grimy socks like she had never seen work clothes before.

"You never took your shoes off in my house," she said.

Mum liked shoes left at the door.

"I mean, I know you were working and such, but it would have been nice if you had . . . when you went into the other rooms like . . . it's the carpet . . . just new . . ."

"Just tell them your plans," said Mum with suppressed impatience.

"Well, they are not exactly my plans per say, more the general plans of the committee, and I have been requested, sent, to impose like—on your good selves . . . and you *are* under no obligation as such, but there will be a feeling of gratitude—no money of course, I mean, the committee is as skint as a sterile kangaroo's pouch—"

"What?" said the three of us in unison.

"An empty kangaroo pouch. Spent a lot of my days feeding kangaroos, in the morning before I was off to work. They *can* . . . you know . . . kick, if you don't know what you are doing . . . saw a dingo once."

"Just tell 'em, would you?" snapped Mum.

"Absolutely, yes, right . . ."

Ms Frasier talked of the wall of gratitude and how it was built ("obviously not to last, as you well know"). She talked of the ethos of the wall of gratitude, who designed it, who changed the design, who believed in the ethos (as it definitely wasn't her), and the falling of the wall ("if it was such a bad thing—for it to fall, that is").

"It's a wall!" shouted Mum.

Ms Frasier, unfazed, moved on to how much it would cost to recycle the wall and how much *some* wanted it to stay, but she did sometimes wonder . . . *as we all do* . . .

I made coffee. Helen searched for biscuits, gave up, and began to make cheese and oatcakes as Mum signed where the chutney was—Ms Frasier's favorite.

"Might even shut her up," she mouthed behind her back.

Helen slid a jar of co-op deluxe onion relish in front of Ms Frasier.

Ms Frasier stopped, caught her breath.

"Are you listening?" She faltered.

"Of course," I said. "Sugar?"

She dismissed with her hand.

"So, what do you think?" she said, pausing to blow on her coffee.

"About what?" I said.

"The wall of gratitude," said Ms Frasier.

"Is it up or down? I'm confused." Helen looked at me. "Didn't I fix it?"

"No . . . yes, you did, but that's not quite the point. The point is . . . well, difficult to pinpoint . . ."

"Oh, for heaven's sake, just *say* it!" shouted Mum.

"What? Oh yes . . ."

She sipped.

"Well, go on then!" shouted Mum.

Finally, with Mum on the edge of her seat crunching an oatcake into smithereens and Ms Frasier with a mouthful of cheese, we got the gist of the story . . .

The committee wanted to arrange a celebration day for, as Ms Frasier put it, "wheelchairs and things."

"Disabilities," shouted Mum.

"Exactly," spluttered Ms Frasier, "a Disability Awareness Day, and they wondered about photos of you at the wedding. We could"—she chuckled—"plaster them all over the wall—the wall of gratitude—pending the committee's latest ethos."

She looked from face to face. "Fun, don't you think?"

"Jesus Christ," muttered Mum as Amy walked in with a "what's that about my wedding?"

Ms Frasier opened her mouth to explain, and Mum jumped in with a "nothing, no need to worry."

"There's no need to interrupt," snapped Ms Frasier.

"Isn't there?" said Mum.

"Quite frankly, no. I was only going to compliment Amy on her young man and wondered if he knew about hanging pictures, if he was handy with a hammer."

"What are these two girls, chopped liver?" shouted Mum.

Ms Frasier turned on Mum. "I was looking for a volunteer. The committee's as skint as a sterile marsupial's whatever—we can't pay anyone."

"What?" said Amy.

Mum gestured a *she's mad* with her fingers. Ms Frasier, with an *I saw that* tut, placed her mug on the sink, slipped her shoes on with a "really," and headed for the drive.

Amy, Helen, and I waved her off as Mum scowled at her.

"Bloody woman. Me, disabled—as if."

"What's that you're sitting in?" said Helen. "A toilet seat?"

"This chair doesn't make me disabled any more than a pension makes me a geriatric. I am more than a friggin' wheelchair. I am a storyteller and a card shark," she shouted, "and the last thing I want is photos of me done up like . . . like a Kangaroo's dinner—"

"Dog, Mum."

"—plastered across the community centre. I mean, how will people take my storytelling seriously?"

Chapter Forty-One

FORGIVENESS

Habits: the scaffolding you build your day around.

Amy followed Helen and me into the garage; there wasn't much tidying up to do. I told Helen and Amy to go up to her flat while I finished off.

"Make sure you come up," said Helen. She caught my face and laughed. "Don't look so scared, the flat's not that bad."

"Mum wants us to toast her new home," said Amy.

"Just the one drink," laughed Helen, "don't panic."

I packed away the rest of the tools and headed up to Helen's flat, wondering what sort of state it was in. If the van was anything to go by, a pretty bad one.

I walked in to find Amy and Helen sprawled out on oversized bean-bags, clutching plastic cups of red wine. Between them was a low Japanese-style table with as many scratches as a second-hand cat scratcher. On top of the table, elegantly set around a candle, were a plate of crackers, a block of cheddar, a humming bit of Stilton, oozy Brie, and a selection of recycled-cardboard placemats (which I vaguely remember Helen talking about making), plus one grape.

Helen told me to pour myself one and "pull up a pew."

"Sorry about the grape," she said. "There were a few more."

I looked around.

The last time I saw the bedsit, the floor was covered in overflowing boxes and bulging bin bags; I couldn't find a loo roll, let alone a coffee mug.

Now, it was like a Nordic, minimalist, open-plan space with bugger all in the seating area, apart from the two beanbags that looked like they needed a few drinks to be comfortable in and a small platform with Helen's bed suspended above the lounging area. *Genius.* A cooking area was flooded with light thanks to a new Velux window. It too was empty, like the sort of kitchen someone rarely made anything in apart from coffee and sandwiches.

It looked bigger, lighter, and tidy, the sort of tidy that made you take off your boots and wipe the toilet seat after you used it (not before).

"It's amazing," said Amy.

"Not sure about the kitchen," said Helen. "Work in progress." She laughed.

We both knew she ate mostly with Mum.

"Where is everything?" I stared at the kitchen area; all I could see was a kettle.

"Built in, like a caravan, a spaceship," said Amy, "a Tardis even." She laughed.

Helen patted the other side of her beanbag and handed me a glass.

"All designed to put your Mum off," said Helen. "She took one look and headed for the hills."

Even more genius . . .

I squelched beside Helen, gingerly clutching my wine as I tried to shift into a comfortable hollow. I rolled towards Helen's thigh and giggled. I felt like a student, though I had never been one; neither had Helen, for that matter. But as she sat cross-legged, hair astray, bra tossed to the wind, it seemed as if she was making up for it.

By the time we were onto our third bottle of wine, Helen was really making up for it, choosing music from the good old days and talking about her new drumming passion, while Amy had moved from what a great guy Gary was to what a *dick* her father was.

Helen, thanks to Amy calling her cheese "boggin'," along with her music, switched Barry White to a low hum and began to search through her secret cupboards for anything salty.

I was mesmerized with her ingenuity of design; every bit of space had been used.

I asked her how long it took to create something so well made, and she shrugged, stating that anger had its virtue. "When you're angry with a hammer in your hands, there are two things you can do: smash or create . . ."

Amy didn't hear. She was fingering her mobile; her father had texted, and she seemed torn about answering. Amy had the sort of relationship with her father that Helen called *distant* and Amy called *invisible*.

As Helen pulled streamlined cupboards from nowhere on the search for the elusive bag of nuts she insisted she'd bought, Amy pondered her father. Amy, like Helen, had been tucking into the wine and was talking with no filter on.

"Always thought he was a bit of a twat," said Amy. "But I had no idea that he was a full-blown one."

"You said he was a changed man," said Helen, peering from a vertical pull-out shelf with nothing in it.

"Yeah, well, that was before the wedding," said Amy.

"Families," I muttered.

Amy emptied her glass, listing all the Christmases her invisible Dad had never joined in. "Not one friggin' Christmas."

"He did bring home a couple of pheasant on Christmas Eve once," said Helen.

"He was a stranger to me until Mum left," muttered Amy.

"Dumped it on the table and left for the pub," said Helen, "and we came home to find feathers everywhere thanks to that cat." She closed a cupboard. "The cat threw up, and wasn't right for days."

"See what I mean, a twat," said Amy.

Helen pulled out a drawer, shuffled about inside, then closed it.

"You'd be surprised how far feathers can spread," she muttered.

"My Mum hates pheasant, she'd have gladly fed it to the cat," I said, filling up Amy's and my glasses.

"I mean, he only paid for that wedding to put on *The Henry Show*.

It was all about him," said Amy. "'Nothing but the best for my daughter' is actually nothing but the best for big fat Henry."

"I wouldn't call him fat," muttered Helen, now staring into her empty fridge for the fourth time.

"He ruined my day," huffed Amy. "I'll never forgive him."

"Janice and Janet reckon he wanted to make you like him," I said.

"In Lycra?" said Amy. "I think it was that Janet and Janice he was trying to impress."

"Forget the Lycra, there's more to Henry than Lycra." Helen gestured with her empty glass. "He is a man who learnt to salsa to impress his daughter."

"I thought you hated him," I said.

Helen flopped onto Amy's beanbag and snuggled next to her daughter. "Hate is fluid."

She opened another bottle.

"Fluid?" said Amy.

"Yes, it comes and goes . . ." She paused for thought. "Sometimes I feel nothing, other times sorry for him, and yet other times—I don't know." She sighed. "He was never dull."

"Families," I said. "You can't choose 'em, you can't live with 'em, and you can't leave 'em . . . you're fucking stuck with 'em."

"I mean, I had no idea that he was jealous of me," said Helen.

"I didn't either," said Amy.

"One of my pals hated her dad," said Helen. "She bossed him about when he was ill, shouted at him when he didn't do what she said. They had an epic row, and do you know what? He died . . . without speaking to her. They never made up."

She touched her daughter's arm.

"Wouldn't you hate that?"

Amy glumly looked at her phone.

Helen's face lit up; she reached for her handbag and pulled out a bag of nuts. "Peanut?" she said.

Amy, dialing, left the room. "Dad?"

Helen tossed the bag of peanuts at me, eased herself up from Amy's beanbag, and turned Barry White up.

She flopped beside me and snuggled in.

I put my arm around her shoulder and patted her. Helen's kindness never ceased to amaze me. All the conversations we had had about Henry, how he had treated her. On her good days, she called their marriage colorful; on bad days, she swore worse than Mum . . .

"That was a nice thing you did," I said with another pat.

"He's her father," muttered Helen, then fell asleep.

EPILOGUE

A few days later, I woke up and looked at Steven's familiar face with a huge sense of comfort and closeness. After the codpiece incident, the darkness had begun to vanish, and the mornings were bliss to me again.

There is something about looking at the same sleeping face in the morning that gives the day a purpose, something to get up to, even if it is just to make that sleeping face a cup of coffee.

It's hard to find words to describe the delicious feeling of belonging, sharing, knowing that you're not alone, especially in the dark hours of the early morning. Steven's snoring had chased away many bad dreams, as had his long legs that wrapped around mine. Sometimes it was the last thing I wanted—in fact, in my dark period, I felt suffocated—but not now. There is real comfort in gently pushing a leg away.

Mum is not right about many things, but she is right about a sleeping face and the familiar octopus legs that wrap around you in the dark.

"You may moan now," she said, "but when they are no longer there, you'll miss them like a TV remote."

"TV remote?"

"Yes, well, what good is a TV without one?" said Mum.

Mum could be cryptic sometimes, especially after a whisky, and yet other times she was as clear as a glass of water.

"Knowing someone enough not to have to speak is the best thing ever," she said, "and if you're lucky, you will never know what it's like to lose that someone and end up getting through your days with TV repeats, whisky, and your own thoughts—or worse, people who you can't be silent with."

I kissed Steven's forehead and slipped out of bed to feed Baby Bea; she had another cold. I slid her medicine between her lips and, like an expert, cooed her to sleep.

****

Would you like to read more? Helen has a past to hide but can she keep up the pretence? While Beatrice's obsession with the library hits a new low for George...
Book 5 ***The Real Story Of 'O'*** is out now.
For a wee taster just turn the page.

Chapter One -Puss

Not All Cats Lick Cream

George looked at himself in the mirror. He brushed his white hair back, tidied his moustache, and slid a clean hanky into his pocket.

His phone pinged.

"Fancy a dram first?"

He stared at it. "Fancy a dram" was code for many things, "walking rather than driving" being one and "staying over" being the other.

He looked down at his trousers and peered underneath at his underpants. *Better change . . .* He sniffed. *And perhaps . . . a bit of Hugo Boss?*

He rustled through his drawer searching for "something different." George had a drawer full of "something different" which, when he swore he'd never see Beatrice again, he had planned to dispose of, either in a fire or a distant second-hand shop where no one knew him.

He stopped. Was he up for a tussle so soon?

❋

Beatrice's jacket was on the back of her chair. She was excited, although if you saw her, you wouldn't know it. The only emotion Beatrice expressed was anger; anything else was hidden away, rarely seen, except the odd moment when George managed to "get it right in bed."

George was picking her up for the Aces High Club, and she had the sheets changed.

Beatrice looked at her phone like she had done just seconds before . . . no answer. *Bugger him,* she told herself.

She stared out of the window.

"Bugger you," she shouted, and the cat on the sink looked up with a *Me? What have I done?* look.

"Not you," snapped Beatrice. "Friggin' men—he could at least let me know."

Beatrice slid her hand onto Puss's chocolate-brown back as Puss pushed her spine into Beatrice's hand with a purr.

Puss had appeared the night of Amy's wedding, posed at the door like it was her home.

She had been lurking about the drive for days. No one knew where she came from, but everyone did that "isn't she cute" stroking as they passed, and Puss knew it was only a matter of time.

She was skinny, young, and always hanging around the outside tap, licking the drips, dozing under the hedges, with an eye on the door and her ear to the ground.

She was an expert of noise, jumping to attention at the sound of a Sheryl's car or Helen's footsteps and lining up for her "isn't she cute" pat.

And it worked every time.

The first time Puss made her move, she was stopped by Helen with a breathless "Jesus" skid, the second by Sheryl with a "fucking hell" trip.

The third time it was fate, kismet, and Baby Bea.

It was late at night after Amy's wedding. Puss watched Sheryl ease a clinking box from the car as Beatrice wheeled herself down the drive with Baby Bea asleep on her knee and Steven, weighed down with Baby Bea's "I'm staying the night" paraphernalia, trudging behind.

Puss saw her chance; like a silent sphinx by the front door she waited. She had seen the door stick like wet sap, she knew it would need pushing, she had it timed, *like trapping a mouse.*

Sheryl wrestled with the key and went for a foot push; there was a clatter of bottles; the box almost dropped; she gripped it and went for a shoulder shove and grunt.

"Here, let me," said Beatrice.

"I got it, Mum"—*grunt*—"bollocks . . . shit."

"Let me," said Steven, pushing forward.

"I said I've got it," snapped Sheryl with a shove of her shoulders.

The door burst open.

Beatrice, pissed off at the "I've got it" from her stroppy cow of a daughter, crashed her wheelchair into the hallway, jolting to a stop just shy of Sheryl's legs.

"Jesus, Mum!" snapped Sheryl.

Baby Bea jolted awake. She began to wail as Sheryl tried to keep her balance with a box full of wine.

"Fuck's sake," she snapped.

Steven, hearing the "Jesus" and the "fuck," pushed the door wide open, stumbling into the back of Beatrice's wheelchair; Baby Bea's paraphernalia scattered everywhere.

Sheryl swore, Beatrice cursed, and Baby Bea, starving, wailed like a banshee . . .

Puss, like the black flash of the Looney Tunes Roadrunner, zoomed in.

"The cat," shouted Beatrice.

"What cat?" said Steven, who had not been to Beatrice's house for quite some time.

Baby Bea wailed louder.

"The fucking cat in the garden," said Sheryl.

"There's a cat in the garden?" said Steven.

"Not now—he . . . *she* is in here now, probably shitting somewhere," said Beatrice. "Shhhh, baby darling."

"I told you—you shouldn't pat it," said Sheryl.

Baby Bea let out a louder wail.

"Pat it? *You* friggin' *fed* it," said Beatrice. "I said shhhh, baby . . ."

Silence . . .

Puss alighted herself onto the hall side table inches from Baby Bea, landing as soft as a ballerina; even the air wick didn't move.

Baby Bea watched, mesmerised.

Puss blinked at her.

Baby Bea cooed.

Puss whispered a soft meow.

Baby Bea, with an outstretched arm, cooed again, and Puss—the master of seduction—titled her head into the small, round palm of Baby Bea, letting out a low rumble of purrs.

A piece of piss.

After a week of Puss skidding into doorways and staring into windows leaving muddy paws prints, a cat flap was built, bowls of dried cat food filled the corners of the kitchen, and Sheryl now arrived with scraps of chicken.

It was like she had been there for years.

Beatrice stroked Puss, her glass of whisky a few sips down.

"At least you don't have to bother," she muttered. "With men and all that nonsense." She stopped. "Although it's not really nonsense, is it?" She sighed. "It's the tits, isn't it? The absolute tits! The waking up, the coffee . . ." She scratched behind Puss's ear. "And if I play my cards right tonight, maybe . . . what do you reckon, Puss? Coffee in the morning, maybe some morning-afters?"

Puss purred.

"Though we're not going to tell him that, are we?"

Puss looked at her bowl; it was empty.

"Treat 'em mean and keep 'em keen . . ." said Beatrice.

Puss mimed a meow.

Beatrice pulled a packet of cat food from the Puss corner and gave it a shake.

Puss landed by the bowl with a soft thud.

"Yes, keep him on his toes, wanting more," muttered Beatrice, dribbling an excessive number of pellets into Puss's bowl as George pulled up in the drive.

George, a man who had many pasts in many countries, had been happily single most of his life. He had never planned to stay long in Argyll, until he met Beatrice.

For a man past seventy, he wore it well—he was trim but not skinny, more bordering on cuddly. And he had a sense of humour that expanded the range of just about anything; making him laugh was as easy as turning on a tap.

George knew he was a catch, that he could have any single woman in the WRI, but the truth was, he didn't care. George was one of those rare breeds who felt comfortable in his own skin, much to the annoyance of many women.

He was a man who liked his own company. He liked the freedom of doing what he wanted whenever he wanted. In the good old days, there were plenty of women happy with a bit on the side, free and frisky— not now. The women he met now wanted to know when and where and if lubricant was required, or as in one case, if sex was absolutely necessary.

Not Beatrice. She was as keen as he was—which was totally undetectable. Beatrice looked that sort who'd slap a penis under the tap and give it a good wash rather than a good seeing-to. But that is the intrigue of Beatrice: she had as many layers as an onion, most involving anger, until the sweet spot was tickled . . .

George thought about the past few weeks without Beatrice. It had been peaceful, like, funnily enough, his army years. Did he really want to go through all that again?

Was the sweet spot that good?

Sure, taming her added a certain spice to his day, and the gymnastics in bed with a disabled woman had added a certain artistic, creative element to lovemaking.

He had surprised himself *and* Beatrice.

But all this library stuff?

She was like a bull terrier: she just would not let go.

***

On sale at your favourite store.

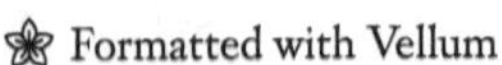 Formatted with Vellum